Murder in the Night

by

Peggy Hargis

PITTSBURGH, PENNSYLVANIA 15238

The contents of this work, including, but not limited to, the accuracy of events, people, and places depicted; opinions expressed; permission to use previously published materials included; and any advice given or actions advocated are solely the responsibility of the author, who assumes all liability for said work and indemnifies the publisher against any claims stemming from publication of the work.

All Rights Reserved
Copyright © 2022 by Peggy Hargis

No part of this book may be reproduced or transmitted, downloaded, distributed, reverse engineered, or stored in or introduced into any information storage and retrieval system, in any form or by any means, including photocopying and recording, whether electronic or mechanical, now known or hereinafter invented without permission in writing from the publisher.

RoseDog Books
585 Alpha Drive
Suite 103
Pittsburgh, PA 15238
Visit our website at *www.rosedogbookstore.com*

ISBN: 978-1-63937-551-6
eISBN: 978-1-63937-592-9

Chapter One

My name is Alex. I live in my parent's home as they moved to Florida to be with their friends and family. They do not like the winters here much anymore so they decided to move to their winter home there. All my life I had wanted to become a detective or work in the police force and when I got the chance to work as a Detective I took the job. Growing up as a child I had a tough time because of the neighborhood we lived in. Until we finally moved here to West Virginia, that is when I finally was able to be myself. I was bullied at my school before the move, I had so much hate from other students because of my love for different cultures and my beliefs, that my parents decided to move me to a different place which was a better school, a better area and I made many friends. My sister who is older lives out on her own and has a family. She has done well growing up. Everyone loves her. I decided to move back into my parent's house when they decided that they had had enough of the cold winter months and wanted to move south to stay where it was much warmer. I go there for Christmas to visit for a break if I can.

I work as a detective in West Virginia. I work under Max Lee who runs the office. He is also my partner. He likes how I think and my expertise. Max is from Korea and moved here when he was fifteen with his parents. Max lives in an apartment up on the Westside with a pool, and we are all getting together on Saturday at the beach. He lives alone and has never been married. He claims that he is too busy to settle down and have a family. But he does not know that I have feelings for him but I am not able to show it because I do not want to lose him as a partner.

PEGGY HARGIS

Today was a cold rainy day as I got up out of bed and had to turn up the heat to warm up the house. I climbed back in bed just to stay warm as I have today off and have to do errands and laundry. I turn on the TV to watch the news. The lady was giving the weather report. It will be at a high of 68 degrees. In other news there was an armed robbery at a local bank, the robbers broke in during the night but they left a clue, one of the robbers has already been arrested. Three more are still on the loose.

Alex finished up the last of the laundry and left to go to the store and to the post office to pick up her mail. On her way home her phone rang, it was Max.

Hi Max, what's up?

I was just wondering if you would like to grab a bite to eat? It is my turn to make dinner since I am always usually eating over there. Would you like to meet me at the Diner?

Sure replied Alex, that would be nice. Thanks, let me change and I will be there as soon as I can. It was five-thirty so it would be nice to go out instead of having to make dinner for one. She thought about inviting him over for dinner but she had not had time to plan a meal

Ok, see you in a bit said, Max.

Alex made it home and put the groceries away and then went into her room to change.

After picking out a blue shirt and blue jeans she got dressed and checked her hair. She then headed for the door to leave. She got into her car and drove to the diner. The traffic was light as most of the people were already home or out eating dinner somewhere. It was a beautiful day out still as the sun was still out. As she pulled into the parking lot she saw Max's car and parked next to it and made her way into the Diner.

Max saw Alex walk into the diner and motioned for her to come over. Just order whatever you want, I am going to order a hamburger, fries, and a milkshake.

Alex looked at the menu. She was not sure what to order as she had only been there a few times. A cheeseburger did sound good though.

MURDER IN THE NIGHT

The waitress came over to take their order and then went to put the order in for the cook. She then got their drinks and brought them right out to them leaving them straws at the table.

Max looked nice in a red shirt with black jeans. But then he looks good in anything that he wears. Alex felt a little underdressed but since they were at a Diner she was fine just the way she was.

After dinner would you like to go to see a movie?

Yeah, that would be great. There is a romance one on if you want to go and see that?

Romance? Really? Replied Max. Why not a comedy movie. You know how I feel about Romance movies.

Ok, that is fine, Alex said. We can go and see what is playing.

Chapter Two

It was early in the morning and Alex got up to go to the store to get some groceries. She picked up some flowers that were at the front of the store. She picked up some dinner for the night, something easy, who did not want spaghetti and meatballs. She had a good day off. The sun was out and she had a lot to do.

She paid for her stuff and then put everything in the car and was on her way. On the way home, she stopped off at a coffee place and went through the drive-thru. She ordered a Carmel iced coffee. She needed that with everything that she had to get done. The laundry was backed up from last week. She unloaded the groceries out of her car once she got home and put them all away. She then sorted the laundry and started a load to wash. She also had dishes to do. She had been working late and knew that she needed to get things cleaned up. She then went to put the flowers in a vase. Then the doorbell rang.

Well hello. I did not expect to see you today. I thought you were going to the beach or something.

No, I got a call this morning. So that was a change of plans.

Well, I am sorry your plans got changed, replied Alex.

Max looked at Alex and grinned at her looking at the fresh-cut flowers in a vase on the counter. "New Boyfriend"?

No, I found them in the store and decided to get them to brighten up the room.

Very nice, replied Max. So we have a new case and we have to go and check out the scene of the crime. A store owner was found dead in her office. She had just closed the store and someone must have still been in the store, or she did not lock up after everyone left. The money bag was still there so it was not a robbery. I am wondering if someone had revenge for her. When you are ready we will go.

How awful replied Alex, do they have any suspects yet?

Not sure. I am going to talk to her brother who came back to the store because he had forgotten something. Was surprised to see that there was money still sitting on the desk untouched so he knew it was not a robbery. So let's go. We have a lot of work ahead of us.

Sure. Let's go. Looks like it's going to be a long night. I will redo the laundry later.

Max and Alex arrived at the store and walked in the front door. A few girls were standing around in the store talking and crying. They looked at Alex and Max as they walked over to the girls.

Do you girls work here, asked Max?

Yes, we had just left last night, and then Larry asked us to come in this morning and told us about what happened. He wanted to know if there was anything unusual going on last night. We didn't notice anything except for a blue car that was parked across the road but it appeared that they were just on their phone when we left. So we did not think anything of it.

Do you know what kind of car? Model?

It was a Ford, I'm not sure if it was a Mustang or what but that is what it looked like. I don't know much about cars, replied Nancy.

Ok thank you, can you tell me anything else that you have seen. What did he look like?

He was a white male about in his late 30's. I have never seen him around before. He had dark brown hair, almost black. Very well dressed and nice looking. He was smoking a cigarette and was on his phone when we left.

What is your name?

Nancy. I live right down the road and walk here to work. That is why I took the job because it is close by. I can not afford a car yet. I was saving for one.

Thank you, Nancy, Now does anyone else have any other information?

MURDER IN THE NIGHT

I have seen him in here before with I think his girlfriend but they were arguing when they left. She wanted to buy a dress and they were arguing about the price. My name is Sara.

Thank you, Sara. My name is Max and this is my partner Alex. Thank you both for your information. Can you hang around for a bit longer in case there is anything else we need to ask?

Sure, Nancy said, we can do that.

Ok thank you, said Max.

Max and Alex walked back to the office area where the victim was lying in a pool of blood. Larry came out of the room and said This is my sister. It looks as if she put up a good fight by the way things are knocked around the room. I don't know who could do this to her. We were doing well here and business was booming. She made some of the best dresses there for anyone of any size. She had her staff that made the dresses and other clothing. She did the designs and the workers made the clothes. She even had a layaway plan for those that could not afford to pay for the clothing right away. Larry started sobbing.

Did she have any enemies, asked Alex?

Not that I know of, replied Larry. I am her brother and we have been working on this since we got out of high school. She did not date much because she was always here pursuing her dream. She has always wanted to be a clothing designer and she loved all the fabrics. You can see that most of them are different, not many are the same unless they were ordered that way.

Ok, thank you for your time, replied Alex. Why don't you go and sit down and I will let Max take a look to see what he can find. I will get back to you in a bit and will take a look around myself. Just try to go through the day today ok?

Yeah sure. Seeing her like this is horrible. I don't know who would do anything like this to her. We both worked hard to get where we are today.

I understand. Do you have anyone we can call for you?

My Parents but I don't want them to know right now. They are not good with bad news. I want to find out more information before I upset them. I have to call the staff to let them know not to come in for a few

7

weeks. I just can't be here. What am I going to do now? She did all the designs. I took care of the business end.

Ok well, I will be back after I take a look around in the other office. You stay here, Alex said and walked out of the room.

Max was in the office looking at all the wound marks on the victim when Alex walked back into the room after talking to Larry. Who is our victim, asked Max?

Her name is Lisa, she is Larry's sister. They had the store for nineteen years. It was quite profitable. Max looked at the mark on her neck, it looked like that she might have been strangled at first but all of the other wounds were stab wounds. She bled out but she could have made it if she was not stabbed near the heart. This is one of the worst that I have seen in a long time. Someone was doing this for revenge. Has there been anyone that she had any problems with? Past employee, ex-boyfriend, maybe someone that had a grudge against her?

Not that I know of, replied Larry. She did not have much time to date although she had a boyfriend, they did not see each other that much because of the hours that she put in. She was always here at work even after hours. That was when her new designs came together.

We will get in touch with you when we find out more information. Her body will go to our lab to be looked at so we can see if we can find any evidence. So sorry for your loss.

Thank you, replied Larry, Can you please send back the girls that are out front? I have to talk to them.

Alex and Max went back to the office and went over the information that they had gathered.

Alex, did you notice anything odd about Larry? Like maybe he was hiding something. He did not even seem to be upset that his sister was murdered.

I did notice that he was not even that emotional. We have to interview the staff to see what they know about Lisa and Larry and to see just how they treated each other. Most siblings are more caring about each other unless they have had a falling out before and are not as close. Alex walked

Murder in the Night

over to the board to write the worker's names on the board, this way they can write down notes about what they say about the owners.

Max made some notes in his notebook and decided to make a few phone calls. The two girls that were in the store managed to get their phone numbers to call them and get some more info.

Well, I am going to go home. I will be back first thing in the morning and check around the area to see if anyone has seen anything and to see if they have security cameras.

I noticed one across the road at the Sub shop, why don't we go tomorrow and talk to the owner and also have lunch, that way it won't seem like we are snooping around the area. Maybe the perp lives around here. Max wrote down the information on his notepad about the camera. I hope that they are working and not a fake one.

I do too, replied Alex. This way we can see who the murderer is.

Chapter Three

The next day Alex got to the department early to look at the paperwork to find out what was found and then to go down to the medical lab to see what Jane had found while examining Lisa's body.

The information that was in the bag was a butcher knife that was found outside of the office, it had already been checked for fingerprints. There was none. The killer must have worn gloves to kill her with. All the information in the report was that there were no fingerprints found, not even on the back door that was found unlocked.

Max came in with coffee and handed one to Alex. Have you found anything yet?

No, there is not much to go on here. No fingerprints, no traces of hair except for Larry's but he was always in the office so we could not put that towards the evidence. This job was very clean, which means that we have a professional killer. Let's go and check to see what Jane found out from the autopsy. We already know what killed her but hopefully, there is something under her fingernails.

Hi Jane, Have you found anything yet asked Max?

Not yet, Max, everything is clean even under the fingernails. This person knows what they are doing. They are professionals.

No clues in the office where she was killed either replied Alex. No fingerprints, no nothing. The only thing that we might be able to get anything from is the camera across the street facing the Clothing store.

Remember the girl that was found last year murdered, the same thing. No clues were found there either. She was outside, no tracks because she was found at a vacant lot. And also happened at night. She was a mile from home. Max rubbed his head wondering if it was the same killer. She was stabbed as well but no weapon was found.

She was twenty years old. Also worked at a clothing store but not at Lisa's. She was found a few counties over in Pipski county. No suspect was caught., this could be our killer. Alex felt a cold chill and said, they can kill again, we have to get on this before they do. More than likely this is a male and not a female unless it was someone that they both knew.

Yes, I was looking over that the other day as I have it filed in my filing cabinet.

Max and Alex drove back to the shop to talk to Larry. Alex had noticed that there were different types of clothing hanging on the racks in the store. Prom Dresses, Bridesmaid dresses, and many other types of clothing. A sign saying Made to order hung on the wall. Lisa had a great little company with all types of clothing even for the bigger women in mind with very tasteful designs. She loved everything that she made.

Larry was on the phone when Max walked in. Larry was telling someone to not come in tomorrow. They will try to reopen next week. He told the other person on the phone about Lisa's Passing but did not want to go into exactly what happened. He hung up the phone and looked at Max. This is just so hard to grasp, he said to Max.

Max leaned up against the door frame and looked at Larry. He noticed that he had been crying and not wanting to answer any more questions.

Larry would have to figure out if he would want to keep the store open or close it after doing a going out of business sale. Knowing that his sister was killed in her office, would he be able to still keep the store open? Many people that have this happen usually close the business or no longer want to work there. Too many memories.

Max looked at Larry and pulled out a card for him to call him if he had any other information or questions, to go home and try to get some rest. Once her body is released you can plan her funeral. I will go over tomorrow morning to see just what is found. She has been there for nineteen years and is very good at what she does if there is anything found

MURDER IN THE NIGHT

on the body or inside. We know how she died but Jane will find out new information.

Larry got up and pushed his chair back in under the desk and Max moved away from the door to let Larry out of the office and followed him. They went to Lisa's office There was still a lot of blood on the floor.

Max and Alex went to the sub shop across the road. The store was closed so they were not able to check out the camera.

They both went back to the department and put what little information that they had into the computer and put the paperwork into the file.

Ok well, I guess that is all we have for now. Let's go for the day. We can pick up where we left off tomorrow.

Chapter Four

The next morning Alex arrived at the office with coffee. Good morning Max, anything new today?

Well, the body is at the coroner's where she has been going over the body and found about 26 stab wounds all over. So we were close to the number of stab wounds that we found. But who would do this to someone? What state of mind were they in? What did she do that was so bad that they went into overdrive? Max just had a bad feeling about this case.

Alex handed Max his coffee. Well, do we want to go back to the shop to see if Larry is there?

We could deliver the news about what Jane had found. Not much more than what we had already told him before. But let's check out to see what he is up to. If there is no one else that he can think of then who could it be? Max did not feel right about this murder and someone knew something and they were not talking.

They locked up the office and drove over to the shop. Larry is going to get tired of seeing us. Alex was sure that they were going to scare him off if they kept asking him questions.

Yes but maybe he had remembered something. Max needed to ask him some more questions. There is just not enough information yet.

Then wouldn't he call? Asked Alex.

Yeah, you would think so. But maybe he is hiding something. Max was determined that Larry had something to hide.

Well ok then let's take a ride over there. Most people have come up with a list by now.

Max and Alex got out of the car and walked into the store. The sign on the store said the store was closed due to a family death. But many people already knew what had happened as it was all over the news this morning.

Larry was in the back and he was making out the payroll for the employees for the week. He looked up and saw Max and Alex at the doorway.

Sorry to bother you, said Max but we have a few questions to ask. Just to find out Lisa's background. A list of friends that she may have had and boyfriends. Just so that we could rule them out. Hopefully, we find a suspect soon and get them locked up. I feel that this is not going to be an easy case.

Larry handed Max a list of everyone that Lisa knew. Circled the person of interest because he was sure that he was her killer.

Why do you feel that these two could be her killer?

One is her ex-boyfriend Robert Clark. He wanted her to close up shop and move with him to Florida. She worked all her life to make this store happen. It has been her dream since she was a little girl. She was not about to just close down and move away.

Who is this other person Larry?

It's Amy Smith. She used to work for Lisa but she fired her because She was stealing money and clothing. She had denied doing it at all but then she had also threatened Lisa because she was fired. She did not need anything else going on her criminal record. She has also been arrested for drugs.

Ok is there anyone else that you can think of asked Max?

Not that I can think of right now replied Larry. But if there is, I will write their names down. Right now I have to plan her funeral once her body is released and I have to contact the Funeral home that we use. I never imagined that we would be burying her before our parents. We still have to buy a plot because we figured that she would eventually get married and will be buried next to her husband but we did not make it that far. Not fair because she never got to have children, get married, or even have a life but her life was doing what she loved and that was making clothes. My parents had always wanted to have grandchildren. Now it's up to me to give them that. I am not in a hurry to get married and have kids. I have not found the

MURDER IN THE NIGHT

right person yet. Lisa was my best friend. We had a lot in common and loved what we were doing.

Ok well, we will go for now and get right on this after we go to the hospital to talk to the medical examiner. Please call us with any other information or if you have any other questions.

Thank you, replied Larry. I will. I appreciate all your help and I do hope you find who did this to my sister.

Thank you for your time, Larry, Max then turned to leave. Alex was waiting out in the store looking around.

Did you find anything you wanted Alex?

There are some nice things here. She had a talent for clothes. These are really nice and great prices.

Well, we will be back and hopefully, it will be open so you can buy some clothes then. Max turned and walked towards the door and opened the door for Alex.

Thank you, Max, you're a true gentleman.

Max and Alex stopped by to see Jane who was checking over Lisa's body to see just what she had found.

Hi Jane, What did you find?

I did a thorough examination on her and found that most of the stab wounds were superficial and a few deep wounds, but the one that did the final blow was to the lung cavity. That might have been the first one that the killer had inflicted on her and then was tired making the rest of them superficial. One stab wound was close to the heart but did not enter the heart. It did however hit the main artery which she had also bled out.

Well thank you, Jane, I thought for sure it was the stab to the heart that did her in. But still, it's sad to know that she had to suffer so much pain during this time.

She did take a while before she passed and bled out. I would say maybe two hours at the most. So her attacker really had it in for her and didn't care that she suffered through this, said Jane.

Ok well, we are going to go and we need a copy of the report so that we can put it in her file.

I can give you that right now, replied Jane.

Thank you, Max said, that would be great. This way we do not have to come back for it. Next is the funeral.

Do you have any suspects yet?

Yes, two as we are going to bring them in for questioning. I just hope that one of them is the suspect. Otherwise, we are going to have to be longer trying to find out who the killer is. Alex moved towards the door and said goodbye and walked out.

Thanks again, replied Max.

Jane handed him the report and Max left.

Max went back to the department and dropped Alex off and then left. He had to go and do some errands.

Alex went in to look upon the computer the two names that Larry had given to them and to see where they lived. They wanted to stop out and pick them up for questioning.

Alex's phone rang, it was Max. Hello Max.

Would you want to go out for lunch? I will pick you up.

Sure that sounds good. I found one address for Robert Clark. We can check to see if he is home later.

What about Amy Smith? Anything on her?

No, not yet. I am still looking though. I will see you when you get here.

Ok great, see you soon. I am on my way.

Max and Alex went to the beach, there is a nice restaurant there that they both like to go to and eat at. The place was quiet so it would be a good time to sit and talk about the suspects.

The waitress brought over two menus and got their drink order and left.

So where does Robert live? asked Max.

Out on Pine Street. Not far from here. We can see if he is home. Alex checked her phone on maps and saw that his house is 10 minutes from where they were.

So are you ready to order? Asked the waitress.

Yes, I will have the fish and chips, replied Max.

I will have the same, Alex said. It really looks good on the menu. I hope

MURDER IN THE NIGHT

that it is as good as it looks. I have heard that they have really good food here. I have only been here once but that was a while ago.

You should try their Mac and cheese, that is really good.

Can we order that and share it? Asked Alex?

Sure why not, one order of the Mac and cheese as well. Max loved their mac and cheese.

Very well replied the Waitress.

The waitress came back with their drinks.

So did you find the phone number with the address? Asked Max.

No, I was not able to find that but we can get that when we bring him in to talk to him, replied Alex.

After they ate lunch Alex paid the bill and they left to go find Robert at his home to bring him in for questioning. They got in the car and watched the people on the beach. Many people were in the water swimming and having a great time. She wished that she was able to enjoy the summer at times but this was her job and she knew that she had to keep at it even though she wished that she was able to go on a vacation and enjoy the beach. Maybe one weekend.

Max pulled into the driveway at the address that Alex had given him. A car was in the driveway so hopefully, he was at home. Max and Alex both got out of the car and walked up the sidewalk and up the steps to the front door. Knocking on the door Max could hear the TV on. The door opened and Robert stood at the door.

Hi, are you Robert?

Yes I am

We are here to talk to you about Lisa, we need you to come down to the department and fill out a statement.

Yeah, I can do that. Let me shut the TV and lock up the house They all walked back to the car and got in and drove back to the department. Max had them all go to his office so that they could talk in private. People often talk more if they are in a private area.

Have you found out who killed her yet? I know that I am one of the suspects as it is normal but I didn't do it. I loved her and I was heartbroken that she would not move to Florida with me but I understood. She worked hard to open that shop and it was her life. I had just hoped that she would open one in Florida. We had talked about it and she said that she would think about it. Now she is dead and I am even more heartbroken. I had wanted to marry her but I had obligations in Florida. I was offered a better job there and that is why I wanted to move.

Do you know of anyone else that would want to kill Lisa and why? Asked Alex.

The only person that had a bad temper against her was Amy Smith. She was good at what she did but she also stole from Lisa. Then when she threatened her I was there that night and I saw how mad she was at her. She has a record for drugs and theft but Lisa knew that and wanted to give her a second chance. After that, she regretted doing so. The phone calls started coming in and the person would hang up after Lisa would answer. She was afraid to leave one night and called me and I came in and walked her out to her car after she locked up. Finally, Lisa was able to feel safe again as months passed and then they started up again. She felt that it would just be over soon but we were wrong. That night that she was murdered I saw her sitting out front just looking at the store, it was dark inside. I happened to drive by and thought that Lisa must have gotten a ride home with her brother because his car was gone and she was not answering her phone when I called to check on her.

So how do we know that you did not do it since you were in the area that night? What were you doing there?

When she did not answer her phone I went by and saw that the store was already dark inside so I figured that she had already locked up, I know what it looks like but I would never hurt her.

Is there anything else you would like to share with us before we bring you back home since we already have your statement? What about her brother? How well did they get along?

Robert looked at Max and replied, they seemed to get along but not always. Sometimes he was mad because he was there just as much as she was but he did not make as much as she did. She was the brains of the company. She did all of the designs to the clothing that she did. Her workers did a great job at following orders on what she wanted and to what colors she wanted. Her prom dresses were so popular, each one was different.

Ok well thank you for your time Robert, we will take this information and put it into the system to keep on file. Alex, will you drop Robert back at his place?

Sure I can do that. Then I will pick up some coffee while we process all of this.

Robert and Alex left and Max went to work at putting all of the information into the computer with the other information that he has stored since the murder. Wonder why Larry would get mad because he was making less, he was not the creator of the clothes yet he wanted the same pay. Lisa had put all of her savings into the shop and took out a loan for the building.

Alex got back to Robert's place and told him that she appreciated his cooperation for coming down and talking to them.

Robert opened the door and got out and said well if you find out who did it he wanted to know because he loved her and hated himself for not being there to protect her. She really showed him what love is and now he will never be able to get her back. He would have done anything to be able to go back and tell her that he would not go because she was worth staying for.

Alex left knowing that Robert could not have killed Lisa because she felt that he was telling the truth. The more that she thought about it the more that she knew that Amy was guilty and definitely had a motive for doing it and that was to get back at her for firing her in front of everyone in the back area with the employees around. People talked about that for a few months after and it finally died down so this is why she was so mad about Lisa and really wanted to get back at her for it. But Robert still had to be on the list of suspects until it was final.

22

Chapter Five

Lisa's funeral was on a Saturday a week after her murder. Family members had to be notified so that they could make arrangements to come to it. Alex and Max came to the calling hours and waited out back to see who showed up. Many family and friends showed up to show their respects. Larry and his parents stood up by the casket and talked to everyone that came up to show their respect.

Then Larry walked away for a while and Max had gone to see just what he was up to. He walked outside and was on his phone talking to someone. Max could only make out some of the phone conversations which Larry and the other person were talking about in the shop. Larry has plans to close it and sell everything in it. He said that he was going to give his parents part of the money and then he was leaving to go to California. Larry then hung up the phone and walked around out back behind the funeral home and talked to family members that were standing outside.

Max went back inside and stood next to Alex, they sat in the back of the service area. A woman walked in and sat down. She did not go up to the casket or even talk to anyone in the family. She stayed for a half-hour and then left. She did not want to be noticed.

Robert showed up and sat down, he was not able to go up to the casket. He still could not believe that she was gone. He saw her parents up in the front row but could not bring himself to go up and talk to them. This is all so sad to know that a sweet innocent woman had passed in such a bad way.

Alex followed her outside to see who it was but she left in a hurry. Alex went in to look at the guest book to see if she had signed in and there was no one by the name of Amy Smith. She walked back in and sat down next to Max.

After the funeral, everyone went out to the gravesite. Max and Alex stopped out to pay their respects. Usually, the suspects wait until the funeral is over and go out to the gravesite after. Max and Alex stayed in the back and looked around the area but did not see anyone at that time.

After everyone had left Max and Alex waited in their car. Someone peered from behind a tree as they walked to the gravesite.

It's the same woman that was at the funeral, replied Alex. I bet that is Amy.

That is what I am thinking of. She must have wanted to see where she was being buried. Let's go and find out.

They both walked over to her without being noticed.

Hello, are you a friend of Lisa's

Amy quickly turned around startled and did not know what to say. I was just here visiting my grandmother who is buried over there. I thought that I knew someone at the funeral.

You were at the funeral earlier, I saw you walk out. What is your name? Asked Alex.

My name is …. Amy could not say her real name so she made up one. It's Melissa.

Well Melissa, how do you know the deceased?

I don't. I saw the obituary in the paper and seen that it was the woman that owned the clothes shop.

Well thank you for talking to us, replied Alex. Have a great day, Melissa.

Amy turned and walked away towards her car and got in. Max and Alex followed.

Amy pulled into a little cottage near the beach and got out and walked in. But what they did not know was that it was a rental that Amy had rented for the week.

Well, at least we know where she is staying. They waited an hour before deciding to leave, they wrote down the address so that they would remember where she was staying.

MURDER IN THE NIGHT

Back at the department Max and Alex sat down in Max's office. The file was on his desk and they added the report and Amy's address to it. We still need to find out where she was the night of the murder.

We already know that Robert had gone by the shop when he did not get an answer. If there is a camera we can find out just when he was there. Alex had remembered that she saw a camera on the store across the street. But is it a working camera?

Let's go and check it out to see if there is a camera there and then go home for the day. Nothing much we can do today anyways. Max got up and walked out the door and locked up as everyone else had left.

I will meet you there, said Alex.

At the store they saw a camera, Larry was at the shop, and Lisa's car was gone. There was not much business going on there as it was dinner time. They walked into the store which sold cards and gifts. It was a cute little store. There was someone working behind the counter pricing more items that just came in.

Excuse me, said Alex, are you the manager?

The girl behind the counter said, no I am her daughter, Megan.

OK well is the camera outside working? We would like to see footage from last week on Friday. I am Alex and this is Max. We are detectives and we need to check your camera.

Sure I can find that for you. My mom is outback. I will get her to find it for you. Follow me.

Thank you. We need it after nine pm that night. Max was sure he would see Robert doing more than just driving by.

Hey Mom, can you bring up the footage from last Friday from the camera out front. I have two detectives here to look at it.

Sure. Is this about the store owner that was murdered?

Yes, it is. We have to see if there is any footage to see if we can see if anyone entered through the front. Max had hoped that it picked up something because there were no cameras out back behind the shop. He had already checked.

The store owner brought up the footage and they watched it and saw a car come driving through that matched Roberts car. See that must be

25

Robert there. He slowed down and then stopped. He pulled in out front and checked the front door but it was locked. So he got back in his car and drove off. So his story matched what he said.

As they watched there was a light that came on in the store and they could see some movement but they were not able to make out who it was. Then the light went off and nothing so whoever was in the store must have gone out the back. But what were they doing in the store?

I am sure that was not Lisa doing something before going back to the office. Larry's car was gone so it was not him. Could it be Lisa and maybe she had heard something out in the shop so she had gone out to check.

Let's rewind it, is there any way that we can get it to zoom in?

Yes, I can do that? Megan came over to zoom in because she knew how to do that. She was more advanced with the camera than her mom. But still, they were not able to make out who it was, just that it was a female that was walking around in the store, they grabbed what looked like a piece of clothing off of the shelf and walked back to the back of the store then the lights went off. Nothing was to be seen for the rest of the night until morning when they were called in to check the scene.

Ok well thank you and if you find out anything else if anyone says anything please give us a call.

I will let you know, Megan took the card and put it on the desk. We are not here as long as the shop is open, we leave before it gets dark. We do not like to be here after dark. Just too risky.

Is this a bad area? Asked Max.

It was at one time but it has been much better but I just do not want to be here if it does happen. Besides, we do not like driving home after dark to go home. So we usually close the store at seven pm. Not much business at that time anyway.

Well again thank you for your time. It was much appreciated. Max turned and walked towards the front and Alex followed.

Well so much for getting anything else from that night. But who was the female that was on the camera? Must have been Lisa. She might have been in her office and was still alive when Robert called but why did she not answer his call?

Maybe she was mad at him or did not want to talk to him, replied Max. I know how women can be.

Oh really? And just how many women have you been with? Alex asked jokingly.

A few. I just do not have time that they want me to be with them. I have not found anyone that understands me. My job comes first. You're the only one that understands because we are always working together. We really need to take some time off.

I agree we really do, we have been working way too hard with what we do. Someone else is just going to have to take over for a few weeks. What are you going to do?

I don't know, replied Max. Maybe I will go somewhere quiet like up in the mountains. I wanted to go home for a few weeks but it really is not enough time to plan. Maybe next year I can do that.

That would be a great thing for you to do. I might plan a trip to Florida to see my parents or maybe I will just stay home and relax. Would be nice to go to a resort. Well I will have to figure that out.

Well, I am going to get something to eat. See you tomorrow. I will bring the coffee this time.

Sounds good Max, replied Alex. See you tomorrow. Get some sleep.

You too. Enjoy. Cuddle up with a good movie or book.

Maybe a bath with some candles. That sounds really good right now. Well, talk to you later. I am heading home.

Alex got home and started the bathwater running. This is what she needed after working long hours all week long. She needed time off from work to just relax. She has not had much time off to do anything for herself and her house needed some spring cleaning. Even though she lives alone it really needs some work done. There is food in the refrigerator that needs to be cleaned out before they become a science project. Tomorrow should only be a half-day hopefully just to watch Amy, see what she does and then they can leave for the rest of the day. Sunday she plans on making a pot roast.

PEGGY HARGIS

Maybe have Max over for dinner. He does not like to cook for himself much. So a home-cooked meal is always welcome for him. Besides, it will give her another chance to be with him instead of working. He hardly ever says no to her cooking.

Chapter Six

Saturday morning Alex arrived at work and saw that Max did pick up coffee for the both of them. They decide to go out and pick up some snacks in the car as they watch to see if Amy leaves the house and to where she goes. Hopefully, she will leave early in the day.

They pull up a few houses away from Amy's house and wait. She comes outside and sits on the porch for a bit then gets up to go back in.

Finally, after a few hours, Amy gets in her car to leave. Max and Alex stay behind her just enough to not really be seen. They drive for over half an hour to a secluded spot. There is a trail. Amy gets out of her car and pulls out a small bag and walks into the area. After she is in the woods, Alex and Max get out and follow her into the woods on the trail, staying just far back enough so that she is not able to see them. Amy goes off of the trail for a brief moment and then comes back out but without the bag.

That's funny, why would she carry back something and then disregard it. She continued on the trail and when they got to the spot Max went to find the bag while Alex continued to follow her. The trail went about a mile around and back out to the road again where she spotted Amy get into her car and turn around to go back in the direction that she came from. A few minutes later Max caught up with her with the bag. Inside they found a knife, about the size of the knife that killed Lisa. Now take this to Jane to see if it matches Lisa's DNA.

They go to the Medical examiner's room and Jane is there and they hand the knife over to her to see if it is a match. Prints will need to be pulled off of the knife if there is any on it to see who they belong to.

Thank you, said Jane. I will get the results back to you on Monday. I have to finish up an autopsy on another body and I have to get it done by today.

That will be fine, replied Max. We won't keep you. Talk to you on Monday. Have a nice weekend.

Both Alex and Max left to go back to the department. On the way there they decided to go by the shop. Larry's car was parked outside and next to it was Amy's car. They waited outside because if they walked inside just to look around it would look like that they were checking up on her. A few minutes later Amy stormed out of the shop and into her car and she took off towards her home. Max and Alex stayed in the car until she was gone and then got out to go inside. They both headed back for Larry's office. He sat behind his desk very angry.

Max said I guess we caught you at a bad time.

Yes, one of our ex-employees was just here and it got a little heated.

We saw Amy storm out of the store and leave in a hurry.

Yes, we never see things eye to eye. We have always butt heads and still do. She got along with Lisa more than she ever did me. Well until she got fired.

What do you mean you still do, has she been here before after she got fired. Max was curious as to why she would still show up at a place where she was fired at.

Yes, a few times. Only to argue with Lisa that she still owed her money. But she was fired for stealing money. She is actually lucky that Lisa did not have her arrested. She did not want that to go on her record. But Amy will not leave it alone. She came here wanting money and I told her no. That is when she stormed out. Her last pay made up for the money that she stole from us but not for the clothing she took.

Well it seems that she would be happy for not being arrested and would just leave you alone, said Alex.

Not her, she has many problems and that is why she has had many jobs. From her application when she filled it out she had listed several jobs down, she never kept any of them over a year. She just does not get along with people. I figured that I would give her a chance and that was a mistake. But I try to give everyone a chance.

Not a lot of people would do that for anyone. Max and Alex realize now that they are dealing with someone with major issues and have to deal with her carefully.

Thank you for talking to us and letting us know. We will keep in touch. Max and Amy left the store to go back to the department as Alex's car is there.

So what are you doing this weekend? Max knew he had nothing planned. Except for maybe hanging out at home for a change. Working as many hours as we do gets tiring. And we get burned out at times. We do not have much staff as we have never been this busy. So I will have to hire a few more people to help work the cases that come in.

I am thinking of making a pot roast tomorrow for dinner. Would you like to come over for dinner and help me eat it? Alex is always looking for a way to get Max over to her place because she likes him so much. He is her ideal man.

I think I can handle that. I will call you tomorrow. Not really sure what is going on. Sometimes one of my friends comes over and we sit and watch the ball game and drink beer but hanging out with you eating pot roast sounds good too.

Ok. Give me a call then I will have it ready anyways. If you decide not to come over I will make you a dish to take home with you Monday.

Sounds great. Thank you. Max was sure he would be over to eat because Alex knows how to cook. Her cooking is great and she should have been a chef instead of a detective.

Ok well, I am off to the grocery store and then home to get some cleaning done and to relax. A glass of nice wine is always great when cleaning the house. And good music.

After the store shopping and getting gas Alex headed home to start working on the house. The first thing is to get rid of the food that is no longer any good in the refrigerator so it was time to clean out what I call Petri dishes. Eating for one and not being home a lot I just do not get my

PEGGY HARGIS

leftovers eaten in time. This is why I need to start bringing in leftovers for Max. It's actually healthier than frozen dinners.

Chapter Seven

Sunday mornings are pretty much laid-back lazy days. It's a day of rest. Alex got up and put dinner in the crockpot. Then with the coffee brewing, she grabbed a cup out of the cabinet and made herself a cup of coffee. She then went to the front porch to get the paper. Another store had been robbed on Saturday night. Thousands of dollars in merchandise have been taken. This is the third one within a week. We have never had this many problems in our little town to even be concerned about. Now everyone is going to be concerned. First murder and now this. We have to see if anyone new has moved into the area. Or near the area as they could be coming over after hours when the stores close and just break in. Which could be a new suspect in our murder case.

The phone rings and Alex sees that it is Max. Hi Max. How are you today?

I am good, Just got done reading the paper and saw that there was another robbery. It's also on the news.

I am thinking that it is someone not in the area. But where are they coming from? We have no clue as to how old or what we are dealing with. Could even be teenagers. The items stolen have mostly been electronics. That is why I am thinking that it is teenagers.

Well, I just wanted to let you know that I will be over later for dinner. Would you like me to pick up something?

No, I am good. I have everything here that we need. It will be ready around 4 pm. But come on over anytime.

Thank you, Alex. You really know how to take care of me. I need a woman like you. Hope I can find one like you in the future. Right now I am just too busy to make a commitment.

Peggy Hargis

Totally understood, replied Alex. It is hard to find someone that meets the criteria of even remotely becoming a match for either of us. Max really is not ready and neither am I. It's just hard to fit dating or a relationship into the work that we do. Who knows maybe he will think of me as his one girlfriend that he can count on.

Well, I will see you later, I have a few things around here I want to get done before I go anywhere.

Sure, Alex said. See you when you get here.

Alex went back to reading her paper and then checked on dinner. It was smelling pretty good and it was time to add the potatoes. She went to the refrigerator and pulled out a bottle of red wine and poured it into a wine glass and then went and sat down on the couch and turned on the TV.

The doorbell rings and it must be Max. He came early to just hang out and then eat. Dinner smells amazing right now and Alex wants to eat right now but she knows that the potatoes still have to finish cooking.

Hello, thanks for coming over. Dinner will be ready in another half hour. It smells so good now I want to eat. Max stood there in a black shirt and jeans. He also smelled good as well which she liked.

It does smell good. But you're a great cook.

Do you want a glass of wine? I also have Coke.

Wine is good, replied Max. Whatever you are drinking.

Sure, you can go ahead and pick out a movie to watch.

Ok, I can do that. Max checked around on the TV and picked out a movie that was getting ready to come on. We can watch Mrs. Doubtfire.

Oh, I love that movie. Great choice. Alex brought him over his glass of wine. They sat and started watching the movie. She was glad that he was there with her, she enjoyed these moments together.

After the movie, they sat and talked.

Well, that was one of the best dinners that I have had in quite some time. I especially love it when someone else cooks.

Alex smiled, She was glad that he had come over. She put up a bowl for him to take home with him along with another slice of apple pie in another container.

34

MURDER IN THE NIGHT

It was getting late and Max had to leave to go home. Alex gave him his bag of leftovers and smiled, see you tomorrow.

Yes, so who is bringing the coffee tomorrow? Max grinned because he knew the answer. Alex always brought the coffee unless he told her ahead of time that he was bringing it.

I will reply, Alex. Good night and drive safe.

Chapter Eight

Monday morning came and there was a message on the answering machine. Max was sitting at his desk. Alex brought over his coffee and set it down on his desk.

Well, you're not going to believe this, But Amy was found dead in her apartment this morning. She had been found hanging in her bathroom.

What? Well now, what are we going to do? She has to be the one that killed Lisa and killed herself so that she would not have to face trial. Who found her?

A friend of hers. She had gone to check on her, she said that she was supposed to meet her for coffee this morning and she never showed. I talked to her on the phone, she said that she just talked to her last night and she was fine. Her name is Mary. She said that it is not like Amy to do this to herself. She thinks that she was killed and then put there to make it look like suicide. Max took a sip of coffee and was filing a report for Amy's case now. So not only do we have one case but now two. The only suspect left is Robert but then why would he kill her?

I don't know but let's go and find out. Let's ask him some questions. Max got up and grabbed his keys and his coffee and they both walked to the front door, locking it behind them. They really needed a receptionist to keep the office going and to do the paperwork but he just has not found anyone that was reliable to come in and work for him.

They pulled up in front of Robert's house and he was outside mowing his grass. Robert saw them get out of their car and shut off the mower. Now

37

what? He had already told his statement. They still do not think that he killed Lisa?

Hello Robert. How are you, asked Max.

I am fine. What is up now? Asked Robert.

Where were you last night? Alex was really interested now.

I was bowling and then I came home. I bowl at Summer house bowling a few miles from here. Robert was not happy about being a suspect still now he wanted to know what else had happened and why are they coming after him again?

Another suspect was found dead last night, they suspect suicide but we want to rule everything out. Do you know Amy Smith? She used to work for Lisa.

No, not really. Lisa mentioned that she had stolen from her and that she fired her. That was it. Nothing more to say as Lisa never really said much about her. She did not talk much to me about what went on at the store. We hardly went out much, only when the store was slow and that she had Larry close up. She just needed some time away.

Ok well thanks, Robert. Alex believed Robert as he did not seem to be the type to lie or much less kill anyone.

Max and Alex went to Amy's apartment. She was still dressed in her clothes. The paramedics got her down and laid her down on the floor. Max looked at the marks on her neck. It actually looked like there were marks on her neck from being strangled, not from hanging. Do you see this Alex? Asked Max.

Yes, it looks like she died before this and then hung to make it look like suicide. Alex was even more confused now. Oh, now we have two people dead two different ways so do we have two different killers? What were the motives?

Ok well, let's go check with the neighbors to see if they have heard or seen anything.

They first tried the two neighbors on each side of her, one neighbor was not at home and the other opened their door to talk to them, she heard people talking in the hallway.

MURDER IN THE NIGHT

Alex was one to speak as Max had gone to a neighbor across the hall. Hello my name is Alex and I am a detective, did you hear or see anything last night?

Yes, I heard yelling and things falling to the floor last night.

About what time?

It was around midnight. She had just got home and then I heard shouting. But then I always hear someone shouting at all hours of the day and night. This place is full of people that do not abide by the rules. I am looking for another place to live. I have not slept much since I moved in. And I did not talk to her at all because she was weird.

What happened to her? Is she ok?

Well, that is what we are trying to find out and no, she is dead. So you won't have to worry about her disturbing you anymore.

I hate to see anyone die or to be killed. That is awful. I stay to myself and do not talk to anyone around here because I am afraid.

Can you stay with someone for a few days until this blows over?

Yeah, I will do that because I do not want to stay here anymore. Fluffy and I do not feel safe here. She gets nervous when she hears any kind of loud noises.

Ok well lock your door for the meantime and please just pack some clothes and bring someone with you when you come back to help move you out.

Will do. This is my first apartment so I had no idea just what to look for. We have only been here for a month.

Ok well, thanks for your time.

Max came over to Alex as she stood outside the now-closed door. They walked to the end of the hall where it was away from the crime scene.

Well, the neighbor had heard some shouting last night around midnight, then heard some things fall to the floor so we know that there was a struggle. But I did not notice anything that fell over so we know that it must have been a struggle. If it was suicide then she would not have knocked things over.

True. The lady across the hall said that she had seen a man in a baseball hat and overcoat that had forced his way into her apartment. It was not the first time that happened so she did not think much about it. She figured it was one of her boyfriends. Then she heard things that sounded like being thrown around and glass breaking. She heard them arguing and then heard her scream and then nothing. She just did not want to get involved so she just went to bed. I guess I can see why people do not want to get involved though.

There is one more apartment to check. I will go and find out if they heard anything. Max left to go to the other apartment. Alex went back to Amy's apartment.

Alex checked around the apartment to see what else could have been moved or used to strangle her with if this is what was used. Because honestly how does a woman hang herself from the shower curtain rod? This has to be staged to make it look like suicide. If anything the person could have put her in the tub to make it look like she had drowned. But then how would you explain the marks around her neck she thought.

Max came back into the apartment where Alex was at. The forensics were working on checking for fingerprints. What do you think happened Max asked one of the techs?

Strangulation. Just look at the marks, there is no way that she hung herself. Hi, my name is Jack. And you are?

This is Alex, my partner, and my name is Max. She was actually a suspect in a murder case that we are working on. But now our suspect is dead so we have to find out who killed her.

Well, I am sorry that this happened, I met her once a while back but she was not very nice but still, no one deserves this. Jack turned and went back to work.

The paramedics came in to take Amy to the hospital for identification and for verification to find out just what happened to her.

Max and Alex looked around the apartment for a while longer, not really finding much to go on. There was a struggle as there were things knocked off as the neighbor said,

Just before they left they found a piece of paper with an address on it. Well this is something to check out, replied Max.

Let's go and find out what it is. Let's go and get a coffee on the way.

MURDER IN THE NIGHT

Sounds good. Then we can go get something to eat. Max was hungry but then he is always hungry. He loves food.

When they got to the address they found out it was an apartment house.

Does that look like Larry's car? Alex and Max never knew where Larry lived. It was a nice apartment. Max and Alex got out of the car and went up to the apartment and knocked on the door. A few moments later Larry finally answered the door.

We found a slip of paper on Amy's floor at her apartment with this address on it. Do you know why she would have it?

No, I don't. And why are you here asking me? Have you found my sister's killer yet?

We are still working on it. We have a suspect but everything that he has said seems true. We do not believe that he killed your sister.

Then why are you here bothering me? Go do your job. I have been through enough. And why were you at Amy's apartment? Checking to see if maybe she did it? To be honest I think you really need to be doing more research on her. She had it in for my sister since she got fired. Then she comes to the store to harass me.

Look, we just asked you a question. If you did not want her at the office why would she have your address at her apartment? At that time Alex really wanted to bring him in for questioning since he was being a total prick. But in time she knew that they had to have more proof to bring him in and to hold him. If they brought him in now he would give them more problems.

I really do not know and I do not want her here either. Now I will have to make sure I park my car in the garage.

Well, you do not have to worry about that. She was found dead in her apartment today.

Well, that is good. Now you have your killer and we both know that she is the one that did it. She is your only suspect that could have done it. She was crazy.

Alex and Max told him goodbye and that they would keep him up to date on any new information.

41

At the Burger hut, Alex and Max stopped in to get a bite to eat. Then back to the department to go over the new information that they have.

You know I really wanted to punch Larry in the mouth when he got rude. There was no reason for him to be like that but now we definitely have a reason to make him a suspect. And he was not at the shop today? I wonder what the reason is.

We can stop by there on our way back to the department and check it out. Wasn't there something that you wanted to buy anyways, asked Max?

Yes, there is. If it is still there. We can check around and see what is going on.

At the shop, there are no other cars around. Both Max and Alex go up to the door only to find the shop is closed. There was a note on the door that said CLOSED FOR VACATION TIME.

Well, that seems weird as well that he did not mention the shop being closed when we were there at his apartment.

Maybe he did not want us asking him more questions. But I can see why, he did just lose his sister and is probably under a lot of stress.

Oh please, he lost his sister and I am sure he is the one that killed Amy. Probably figured that Amy had killed his sister so he would get back at her and kill her. Alex looked in the window and saw the dress that she wanted.

Ok well, you need to go home and get some rest, you're overtired here. Max went to get in the car to take Alex back to the department.

I don't need to go home. I am perfectly fine. We have to go over the other information that we have.

Back at the department Max and Alex went over the file. Tomorrow they would go and find out what information that Jane has collected from Amy's body. Max was sure that she was killed before and that Jane would find the same information.

So what are you doing later? asked Max.

I really don't know. I guess just relax. I do not feel much like doing anything else. I have the roast for dinner tonight so I do not have to cook. I might even watch a movie. Or just read a book.

MURDER IN THE NIGHT

Sounds good. I am going to relax as well. I have to call my family to see how they are doing. I am going to try to get them through Zoom so we can see each other. I miss being home. I really want to go back to visit. Not to live though. I like it here. And it gives me a reason to go back to visit from time to time. I miss the food there too, you should go and try the street food. It really is great. But some of it I can make here.

That would be nice. You can teach me how to do it. And we can have Korean food night once or twice a month.

Great, I will get with you on that. Maybe next week? Max really has not found anyone that cooks the food like they do in Korea. We can even do Korean Bar-b-que. With some noodles. I will buy all the stuff and bring it over one day early.

Well, I will see you tomorrow. Going to go home now. Get some rest tonight Max.

Alex got home and slipped off her shoes, went to the refrigerator and took out the bottle of wine, got out a wine glass, and poured herself a nice glass of wine. Ahh, finally it will be nice to just sit and relax. Sitting down on the couch and turning on the TV to see what is on. She clicked on the news. Her phone rang, it was her mom in Florida.

Hi, how are you doing Mom?

We are doing well here. Just trying to stay cool, it has been in the '90s here. Thankfully we are able to go in the pool during the day. How are things going with you?

I am ok. Just been busy at work. Have two murder cases to work on. Just when we think that we have figured out who killed one person, that person ends up dead too.

Wow-what happened?

One lady who owned a shop was murdered and found by her brother the next day. We had it down to two suspects, only one I really do not think killed her. But the one that we were looking at ended up dead this morning.

Well, that seems to be a sad case to work on. Two people were killed and now you have to find out who the killer is. It could be anyone.

Yes but hopefully it is one of the people that we have as suspects.

Well, I hope that you're able to figure it out. Anyways your father and I are going to California for a vacation trip. We have friends that live out there and they invited us out to see them.

Awesome, when are you going?

Next month. We are going to fly out. We had thought about driving out and checking out the places as we go through the different states but it will be too long of a drive for us.

Yeah, that will be a long drive. Well, have fun and take pictures of your stay. How long are you going to be gone?

Two weeks. Maybe longer. We really do not have anything going on and we want to do some traveling so this way we can do it. It's a great way for us to enjoy our retirement.

Wish I could go with you but we have the case to close first but anyways have fun. Maybe you will run into a celebrity while you're there.

If I do, I will get their autograph. Maybe even a picture of us together if they will let us.

Well, I am not sure if you can do that. They have bodyguards. I am sure that you will not be able to get close to them.

Well, it never hurts to try right?

No mom it does not and have fun.

Oh, we will.

Chapter Nine

The next day Max was already at work. Early as always. Alex came in with the coffee.

Max looked up and saw Alex. Oh, thank you for the coffee. I need it. I did not sleep well last night thinking about what has happened with Lisa and now Amy. I really do not think that Amy had killed her. She may have been crazy enough to do it but I feel like that someone else did it. But who? Robert does not fit in the puzzle. The only other one that I can think of might be Larry but why would he kill his sister? That just does not seem possible. I am wondering if someone else did it that we do not know about.

Well, it could be. But who? Maybe we should question Larry again to see if he can think of anyone else, there has to be someone else. Unless she was just killed by some random person that might not have even known who she was. What about someone that was released out of prison that lives in the area? Do we have anyone there?

There is one person, he was released just before Lisa was killed. I had read it in the newsletter that I get with people that have been released. We could check him out.

Well, where does he live, and did he even go back there? He might have gone somewhere else. What is the name?

John Smith. I am wondering if it is a relative of Amy's. Max scratched his head and then looked online to see if there is a picture of him listed.

Could be they have the same last name but then there are a ton of people with that last name.

Yeah, that is the only problem with that and John is also popular. There must be at least a hundred John Smiths near here.

How long was he locked up for and for what?

Burglary and carrying a weapon. He even threatened someone before he was locked up. He was in for five years.

Ok well, let's see what Jane has found first, and then we can see if we can track this guy down.

As they gotta see Jane she was just finishing up the report.

What did you find Jane, Max was hoping that it was strangulation as he did not think that she would do suicide.

It was strangulation. There are older marks on her neck as she was still alive but the marks that were made from after was when she was already dead.

So it is what we thought Max said. Someone had killed her first then made it look like she did it. It has to be a male to lift her that height to make it look like a suicide. Unless it was a very strong woman. But from what the neighbors had said, it was a man that was there that night.

True, even I am not able to lift someone up like that. So there goes one suspect, now we just have to find out who killed her. Do you think it was the same person who killed Lisa?

That I do not know, replied Jane. Both were done in different ways. And I agree with your thinking it would have to be a guy to lift her up as they did. Amy weighs one hundred and fifty pounds. Lisa was more than that.

So why would someone kill Amy anyways? Jane asked.

Well, she was not a great person to get to know, I believe that she had a mental illness and was probably not taking any medications for it.

Well, that will do it. Ok well here is your report for your file. I am sorry I could not be of any more help to you.

Thank you, said Max. We have another stop to make to try to find someone. So thank you again and we will see you later. Hopefully not right away again this time.

Back at the department Max and Alex looked up all of the John Smiths and their addresses to find out where they lived and how close that they

MURDER IN THE NIGHT

live. To see who has been arrested. This should narrow down the search quite a bit.

Alex looked a bit and found a John Smith in the area a few blocks down.

Max was able to look up the John Smith that had been listed on the website but the address did not match. There was a picture. Hey, I think I know who that is. I have seen him around before. I think I know where he worked. So let's go to this address that I have for him and see if he is home.

They got into the car and drove over to the address that Max found on the computer. They both got out and went up to the house and knocked on the door. A dog was barking behind the door. No one answered the door. A TV was on and a car was in the driveway. Maybe he went for a walk.

With the dog inside? Let's check around back first in case they are outside, said Alex.

Could be.

They both walked around back and found no one there either.

Well, let's go and check out the other house. Hopefully, we're lucky out there, said Max.

I hope so. I really want to get this done so we can get the killer behind bars before they do it again.

Well, we are not able to arrest anyone without some kind of proof. I think we have one suspect and I think you know who that suspect is.

Yes, I do. He has to be the one that did this to both of them. Both suspects have a possible motive.

At the next house, it was empty. So where is this John Smith anyways?

We can ask the neighbors if they know where he might have moved to.

An older lady was sitting out on her porch drinking coffee. Alex and Max both crossed the street to talk to her. If she sits outside she probably knows everyone on the street.

Hi, said Alex. How are you today?

I am fine. And yourself? I can tell you are not from a round here.

My name is Alex and this is Max. Do you know John Smith that lived across the road?

PEGGY HARGIS

I do not know anyone by that name. There was a woman that lived in the house over there but she moved. A guy used to come and visit her but he did not live there.

Do you know where she moved to?

No, I do not. All I know is that she moved out of state. A few months ago.

Ok thank you, replied Alex. Have a nice day. And if you hear of anything here is my card. Please give me a call.

I will but I don't think I will.

At the department, Alex and Max checked to see if anyone had called. Max had put in an ad for a receptionist. There were a few messages. Max had checked them and called them back while Alex put the other information in the folder. Alex had gone out back to make a pot of coffee. They were going to be there for a few hours trying to figure out where John Smith was. Alex called the prison where he was released to see if there was an address that he was going to. The operator did not have any information.

Well, are you able to send me a photo of him so we know who he is?

I can give you a photo if you want to come and pick it up. I will give you the address.

Alex wrote down the address and then left to go and pick it up. She got in her car and drove to the prison and entered through the front door. Alex stopped at the window in front of the Prison and asked the girl behind the glass for the photo that was left.

Sure right here. I just need you to sign for it.

Ok, sure. Thank you so much.

You're welcome.

Alex left to go back to the department to where Max was and to show him the picture. When she got back she saw Larry's car parked out front. She would have to wait until he left before looking at the picture and what other information was in the envelope.

Max was in his office with Larry. Larry was going over other possible suspects since he found out that Amy was killed. There were a few more people that had a motive to kill both of them. Larry had wanted this to end so he could move on after losing Lisa.

MURDER IN THE NIGHT

Thank you, Larry. I will check these people out. Bring them in for questioning. I really wish this was over as well. So that you and your parents will be at ease knowing that the person responsible will be behind bars.

Larry left the office.

Where did you go?

To the prison to pick up a picture of John Smith.

What? Oh, great news.

Alex took the envelope and both looked at the picture. She recognized him from the store down the road. He used to work there. I shop there all the time. He was always nice to me. I am not sure he is even capable of killing anyone. I don't think we have our man.

Well, let's call it a day and go home. See you back here tomorrow.

Ok well, I am not sure just how much we are going to get done tomorrow. But we can take the day to see what we can find out. I know that he used to go to the park near the store. We can check there and a few other places.

Alex had gone home and opened the refrigerator and took out the bottle of wine. She was almost done with this one and had another one that was cold. The job was rough on her and she needed time to just regroup. To get her mind off of everything and to just leave work at work. She knew that she was in need of a vacation. Someplace to getaway. Something to take her mind off of what has happened. She has nightmares sometimes of the people that she has seen but it is part of the job and she knows that it is important that she finds who did this so that they are not able to do it to anyone else.

Alex turned on the TV and watched the news. The days were going to get cooler in the next few days. It has been really hot out and she wanted to be someplace on the beach. That would be nice.

Later that night the doorbell rang and it was her friend Regina.

Oh wow, Hi, come on in. Alex was very happy to see her friend as she has not seen her in over a month.

Hi, I finally went by your house and saw that you were home. I do not like to bother you because I know that you're busy but when I saw your car

49

I had to stop by. How have you been? I am good, I have been busy with two different murders. I am not able to go into too much detail as of yet because we still do not know who did it. Have a seat I will get you a glass of wine. Are you hungry? We can order out.

No, I am fine, I just ate with another friend of mine.

Oh wow, that is awesome. You can never have too many friends and you are so outgoing. I used to be but my job is very demanding. So I do not get too much time to be with family and friends. My job is my life.

I understand. I miss you and not getting to go and do things together.

Well, what are you doing this weekend? Maybe we can do something then. Alex knew that she needed time off to spend with her best friend. They have been friends for a long time.

That would be great. I am off from work this weekend so we can go and do some shopping. That is what we love to do. A ton of bags and a ton of money missing from our bank accounts.

Yup and I need some new clothes. I have not gone shopping in a while. Oh and my Mom called. Guess where she is going in a few months with Dad?

To Hawaii?

No, but that is a thought. They are going to California to visit friends.

Wow, nice. I wish I could do something like that. But I work so much I just do not have the time. I got a promotion and I am an assistant writer at the office.

That is great news. I always knew you could do it, girl. I have always had faith in you. You were the one with all the good grades in school and the looks. I was surprised that you did not get a homecoming queen. You deserved that. Shoot you were much prettier than that other girl that won.

Well, you know why she won. She gave the judges the time of their life and I was not like that. I do not do things with just any man.

Yes, but she was not just any ordinary woman. She would do it with anyone.

That is true. Alex knew that Mandy would do any of the guys, especially the football team. Even she would do the football team. Well most of them. Most of them looked hot in uniform.

MURDER IN THE NIGHT

So where do you want to go shopping this weekend? At the mall? They have a few new stores that opened. And we could go out for lunch and drinks.

Yes, that would be awesome. Sounds like a fun time. Just what I need to do to forget this week. Then if you want you could stay over Saturday night and we could sit up and talk like we used to. I will make you breakfast Sunday morning. Ok, I am going to put in an order for food and will have it delivered. What are you in the mood for?

Not really been hungry since I ate but I could go for some Chinese.

Ok, I will put in an order and order a few other things.

So what is new with you? Do you have a man in your life yet?

Alex grinned, Well no not really but I really can not talk about it. He does not know that I like him. Or at least I do not think that he does. I do not want to jeopardize our friendship if it does not go well.

I understand that. It happened to me once. But I am married now but we just stay busy with work all the time.

The doorbell rang and it was the food delivery. Alex paid the guy and gave him a tip. She brought the food over to the table and grabbed two plates and some silverware to eat with. Regina got up and went to the table and sat down with her glass of wine and they sat and talked some more about old times while they ate.

A few hours later Regina had left to go home and Alex decided to call it a night and went to bed. She changed into her pajamas and laid down in bed and turned on the TV to watch a movie before falling asleep. Before she knew it, it would be morning again and time to do it all over again.

51

Chapter Ten

Alex got up and got in the shower to get ready for work. It was a little cooler from what it was yesterday. They needed rain but that was not in the forecast at all this week. She was running late and she figured that she would pick up breakfast on the way to work.

Max was in his office when Alex arrived. Happy about the weekend she gave Max his order and went back to her office. She looked online to see if she could find John Smith and put the area that he was in and she actually found something online about him. The address that she had found of his that was recently was nowhere near where the two women were killed. He is in another state now. He must have moved when the lady that he was going to visit at her place had moved to. Maybe they moved together.

Max walked into Alex's office and told her that a few women were coming in today for an interview for the receptionist position. Alex went back to looking online and wrote down some addresses. There were a few more John Smiths that lived in the area and she needed to check them out to verify that he was not in the area.

Hi Max, I am going to run some errands and check on these few addresses to see if John Smith is there. I will be back later on. Good luck with the interviews.

Thanks, Alex. I really do not like interviewing people because I never know just who to pick but we will see who works out. Someone also called and said that they wanted to work with us on these cases.

Great. Now maybe we can stop working so many hours. Alex then turned and walked out the door to go and check out the other places.

PEGGY HARGIS

Alex came back to the Department and found Max talking to a woman about the job. She would have to wait to tell him what she found when she went out to check the other places. She did find John Smith. He answered her questions and she left. He seemed honest enough but she will have to write everything down in the report and go over it with Max.

Finally, Max was done with his last interview and he said that he would call with his final decision. He came into Alex's office to talk to her and to find out what she had found out.

Ok, so I have a file on John Smith. He said that he was working the night that Amy was killed and was not in the area when Lisa was killed. I checked with his job and he is telling the truth. He is a cook at a local diner close by and near his home. He works there as much as he can to earn money because he owes money for bills that he is trying to get caught up in.

So where was he when Lisa was killed? How do we know that he did not do it? Alex, we have to get this done so we can close this case.

I know and I am trying so I checked that out too. He was at a funeral in Tennessee. I checked and he was there. He was a pallbearer. So he is telling the truth so I think we can take him off of the suspect list. But he is the man we were looking for. Alex closed the file and put it in the cabinet.

Ok, so we are back to Robert. Max scratched his head thinking maybe he had hit a dead end. He did not want this to end up a cold case. Several of their cases have ended up being cold cases.

We will have to bring him and Larry in for questioning. Larry just as a precaution because he is the brother and yes we do have to have him checked out too. Alex just did not like having to bring both in so it would have to be done separately so that it would not look like one had turned against the other.

I totally agree. Well, we can do that tomorrow. I will stop by and pick up Larry first in the morning and then we can question Robert later in the afternoon. Put both stories together and see what we can find out.

Well, I will see you tomorrow, I have to go home and get some things done. I will see you tomorrow if we are done here for the day.

Murder in the Night

Sure yes, we can leave for the day. Friday I think that we can go ahead and call it an early weekend. I have some things to do. What are you doing this weekend?

I am spending it with a friend of mine. We have been so busy that we decided to go and do some shopping and stuff and spend the weekend together. She has been my best friend for a long time.

Ok well, see you tomorrow. Max went back to his office and finished up what he was doing and then locked up. He had planned on picking up dinner for himself for the night because he did not feel like cooking.

Alex stopped and got some dinner and picked up a few extra bottles of wine for the weekend. She and Regina had a lot to catch up on. It is always nice to have a girl's day out for once.

Once she got home the phone rang. It was Regina.

Hey, how are you? Regina sounded happy on the other end.

Great, are we still on for this weekend. Alex had hoped that she was not calling to cancel on her. She really needed this girl's time together.

Yes. Of course, we are still on. I just wanted to call and see how your day had gone. Are you home or still at work?

I am at home. Just got home. I picked up more wine this weekend. We are going to have so much fun.

Yes, we are. So did you get to work with your guy today?

Yes, I did but he was interviewing someone for the desk job. We really need someone there to answer the phone and to be there in case someone came in and needed to talk to us. Just someone to be there. And I was busy checking in on another possible suspect but he is no longer a suspect. But at least I solved that part of the case.

I wish I knew more about what was going on. It sounds interesting. Regina really was interested in what Alex does for a living. It never seems boring.

Well, that is the problem. I really am not able to talk about the case just yet until it is over when it is all out in the open and done in court. Alex really wanted to tell her but she was not able to do so. It was part of the job.

I understand, I get it. So what are you doing tonight?

55

Just getting the house ready for the weekend. I have to get my laundry done as I usually do it on the weekends. I am off Friday to get other things done. And to rest before our busy weekend. A Lot of the stores have a big sale this weekend at the mall. It should be a great time.

That would be great. I love sales. I think that all women love sales.

I sure do. Thanks for taking the time to hang out with me this weekend. I miss that. Alex has been wanting to go out with some friends anyways. Girls just understand each other. Men have some clue what is going on but not like friends do. Especially those that have been friends for a long time. And Regina is one that she could trust. She was like a sister.

Ok well, I will let you go. I have to get some work done tonight. I will call you Saturday.

You can call me on Friday if you want. We can check to see what is on sale before we go to the mall.

Yes, that would be fine. I will call you then. Have a great day tomorrow.

Chapter Eleven

The next morning Alex arrived at the department. Max was on the phone calling one of the potential people for the job. She went to her office and put everything down on her desk. She started working on the case and making a report on what she had found out and what the results were from her findings.

Max got up from his desk and went into Alex's office and sat down. Well, we have someone coming in today. So she will be here in an hour. Then we can go and pick up Robert and bring him in for questioning and video the conversation. Then we will bring in Larry after lunch.

Ok, I will call Robert to have him come down to the office. He will come in and talk to us with no problem.

Ok good. I will have to get Madison set up in her office. So go ahead and call Robert to see if he can come in this morning if not call Larry and schedule Robert for this afternoon.

Ok, Alex walked back into her office and closed the door. Sat down and called Robert. He was not at home so she left him a message to call her back. She then called Larry. He could not come in today as he was busy with family matters. Alex got up and went to talk to Max.

Well, change of plans. I called Robert and left a message and we are not able to get Larry in here today.

Ok so call him back and see if you can set up a time on Monday. We need to get this going so we can get this done. Usually, we are done by now. But then we usually do not have two separate murders. The only reason why we are together is that I think that it is the same person. And if we can link that person to the same person then we can finish the case and send it to trial.

I will mark that on my calendar to call him on Monday.

The door opened and Madison walked in. Max went out to greet her. Hello, how are you? Are you Madison?

Yes, I am and I am good thank you for giving me a chance to work for you. I love doing this type of job. I love people and I worked for a doctor's office for twenty-one years until he passed away.

Ok well, this is your desk and the computer is hooked up to the printer over here in the corner. All of the computers are hooked up to it.

Oh, the Maxima 2000 I am used to working with one. The doctor's office had one just like it. That is funny, Maxima and your name is Max.

Yeah, I never thought of it that way but it is funny.

So your responsibility is to answer the calls, set up appointments for us for new clients, and billing the clients. So you will also be in charge of accounting. As you will be collecting payments and putting them in the system and the checks or payment goes to me. I will be making the deposits.

Ok, I know how to do all of that too. I miss doing this kind of work but this will be different as I will be working for detectives instead of a doctor's office and not as busy.

We just feel that the clients can come in at any time or call and we can call them when we get a chance. We will try to get back to them right after you give us the message.

I love this job already. So you both go and do what you need to do. I have this.

Ok great. Since today is your first day, would you like to go out for lunch with us? So we can get to know each other better.

Yes, that would be great. I just need to know do you have a refrigerator and where is your bathroom at?

The kitchen is out back and the bathroom is next to it. There is a coffee maker and microwave as well and a small table with chairs. Max showed her around.

MURDER IN THE NIGHT

Oh, nice. I can bring my lunch then since I will be here all day. Madison was glad of the setup of the kitchen. It is more personal than in a doctor's office. They are only allowed to have certain things.

Or you can go out for lunch when we are here at the office.

Ok, that would be nice once in a while but I mainly like to stay at work and eat when I can. I like to stay busy.

Well, I am sure that you will be busy but some days not so much.

So where would you like to eat?

I don't care. Wherever you like to eat is fine with me. I like everything.

Max locked up and they all got in Max's car and drove to the diner. It has everything there that one would want. We like eating there. It is one of our favorite places.

At the diner, Max parked the car. The place was busy. It was lunchtime so everyone was out for lunch. They had to wait a bit for a table to open up.

As they stood there they saw Larry at a table eating alone. Then a woman came out of the bathroom and came over and sat down with him. They sat and talked, it looked more like a casual lunch together. She had some paperwork that she was going over with Larry.

Ok so maybe it is a business lunch. Alex said that he had a family matter today but that does not look like a family matter. I wonder what is up. What kind of business is he doing? Insurance maybe?

The hostess came over and brought them over to an empty table. Max and Alex sat on one side and Madison on the other. This way they could both talk to her from across the table.

A waitress came over and took their drink order and then left, leaving three menus.

Order what you want, Madison. It's on me. Max looked over the menu and then looked down to where Larry was sitting. Both he and the woman got up and left.

Well, they both left so I wonder what that was all about. I wonder if he is going to keep the shop or sell it. He has the chance now to make whatever salary that he wants now since he is the owner of it. Max was always thinking about things. He has the experience to know what people are thinking when things happen like this. People get greedy.

Alex saw them leave as well. Well, I wonder who that was and what the paperwork was all about. We will have to wait and see if the shop goes up for sale.

Usually, after someone dies everything of theirs is sold and the person who is taking care of the estate takes the money and does what they want with it. Usually goes towards funeral costs. Maybe he is having to sell the shop because of the burial expenses.

Well, that does make sense. And whatever is left they can do what they want with it. Especially when something like this happens suddenly and they are not able to plan for a funeral before someone passes.

The waitress came back with their drinks and took their order. While they sat and waited for lunch they talked more about what they did.

After lunch, they went back to the office so that Max could show Madison where everything is and goes. The case that they are working on now they had gone over to get her up to date on what was going on and what will happen next.

Alex had called Larry on the phone and he answered. Hi Larry, this is Alex. I am sorry to bother you this afternoon but I want to know if you can come in on Monday to talk to us here in the office.

Sure I can come in. What time?

Anytime Monday morning is good for us. We will be here for most of the day.

Well, I can stop down at nine in the morning. I have an appointment after that.

Ok, thanks, that will be great. Have a great weekend. Alex was glad to have been able to get ahold of Larry before she left to go home. She checked the answering machine and no calls from Robert. Hmm well, that is odd. I wonder where he is. I hope he did not decide to bail on us and leave the state. Because that means that we have to go and find him and bring him back and lock him up.

MURDER IN THE NIGHT

Alex went out to talk to Max and to let him know that Larry was coming in on Monday.

Anything on Robert? Max asked.

No, not yet. I will try again on Monday.

Thank you, Alex. We are done for the day. Madison I will see you on Monday at eight. Have a nice weekend. We are not going to be here tomorrow as I have things to do so we are taking a long weekend.

Ok thanks, Max. I will see you then.

Chapter Twelve

Saturday Morning Regina stopped over to go with Alex to the mall. She is spending the weekend with her so she brought a bag to stay the night. They have not done this in over two years. They got in Alex's car and drove to the mall.

The mall was full of people already first thing in the morning with shoppers all over. Christmas would be here before you know it and Alex wanted to get started on shopping early. Right before Christmas, everything goes up because the last-minute shoppers will buy anything.

Alex had a list of places that she wanted to check out so they checked on the mall guide to where all the stores were at that they had to go to. Alex and Regina wrote all of the floors and numbers that the stores were at to make their shopping easier.

After a while of shopping, they decided to stop and get some lunch.

Well, how much have you spent so far? Alex asked

Over two hundred dollars. I got the kids all done but now I have to figure out what to get the adults.

I think I spent five hundred already. I only have adults to buy for and my parents I have to send their gifts down. But I am sending them gift cards to keep the cost of shipping down. Besides, they would rather have gift cards. They do not need too much of anything else as they always tell me that they have everything that they need.

Well, that is good. The kids are funny. They have written Santa a list of stuff that they want. I tell their parents what I got and they get a gift of something else that they want and put Sants's name on it.

Do they still believe in Santa? Asked Regina.

Well, the five-year-old niece does. She is cute. Then I have to go shopping with Max because he does not know what to get people. He just likes the company I think. He has his parents here but they have gone back to South Korea for a visit and have been there for over a month. Now Max is wanting to go and visit and I would love to go with him to see where he grew up. I have seen many different things in South Korea online and I really want to go.

Wow, so when are you going to go?

Next year I hope to go there. But we will see. Might go when Max goes and he can show me around but then I want to go alone because he has his family to see.

Well, it sounds like fun. So when you get to go have fun. I wish I could go and visit places but I just do not have the time or money to go to them. Maybe one day I will get to go.

Where do you want to go, asked Alex.

I really want to go to Paris. It just looks so amazing there. Regina smiled and then laughed, well it is just a want. Not like it is really going to happen.

You never know, said Alex. It could happen. And it should happen. You and your husband need to make a trip there. You only have one life and now is your chance to get to go. Save your money and go. Do it while you can.

Your right replied Regina. We have been working our whole life, we have no children together and we do not want any because we work too much but we really do need a vacation like this. So maybe we will check it out online to plan a vacation and to see what packages are out there and what we have to save for.

Sounds great. You never know what can happen, you really need to do this together. And take some time to spend together. You can't work all your life and never have time for each other.

Your right, Regina said. It's hard enough to get time together during the week and when the weekend comes we just do not feel like doing anything. We might go out to eat and that is it. It is too much to go out and just have fun.

MURDER IN THE NIGHT

Well, sometimes you have to make time. Plan on a trip to go somewhere. You both can take some time for yourselves. If you don't then you really do not have much of a marriage.

It is already there. We just do not talk like we used to. We both come home from work, I go out and make dinner and he sits down and watches TV, and then after everything is done I go up to bed. He comes up later on.

See you need to make time. You're letting your work get in the way.

I know but we have done it for so long we just got used to it.

Come on, take a Friday off and start the weekend right. Both of you. While it is still nice weather.

Ok, I will look up hotels online. Will you help me?

Yes, I will be happy to help you look for a vacation spot. Why not do a week?

Well, I am not sure. I don't think that Rick will want to take off for the whole weekend, much less the week.

Ok well, we can start with the weekend.

Now let's finish up our shopping. We still have a few more stores to go to. Alex was ready to get done and get home. She had the night planned for the both of them. And now they have to plan for a weekend getaway for Regina and Rick.

Back at the house Alex and Regina went into the house and Alex got out two wine glasses and a bottle of wine. Pouring the wine and handing a glass to Regina she asked, so what kind of trip are you looking to do?" Romance or fun.

Romance would be good so that we can get back to being ourselves again.

Ok so let's look online to see what we can find.

Sounds like fun.

Alex grabbed her computer and opened it up and brought up Romantic getaways. Let's look for something that is at least a few hours away. Somewhere near the beach ok?

Yes, that would be great.

Ok great, let's see what they have.

Here are some Bed and Breakfast places to stay at. Where do you want to stay? Hotel, Inn, Cabin, or Bed and Breakfast.

Well, maybe we could do a cabin. And it really does not have to be near the beach. We just need to get away.

Ok, so Cabin would be ideal for a Romantic Getaway. Here is one that is nice, a few bedrooms, a deck, and a private jacuzzi. It even has a grill so you can cook out on the deck. Plus it is close to a casino so you can go there and win some money.

That does sound really nice. How much?

Alex looked and checked it out for two nights. Two hundred and sixty dollars for both nights.

Great. Let's book it.

After booking the night they decided to watch a movie and talk about other things and then went to bed. Both feeling a little drunk from the wine they went to sleep with no problem.

The next morning Alex got up and made a pot of coffee. Not long after Regina got up.

I smelled the coffee and heard you out and about here so I got up.

I was going to make some muffins too.

I will help. What kind do you have? Regina was hungry after yesterday. They were so busy last night that they forgot to eat.

I have blueberries, said Alex.

Oh yes, my favorite.

Great. I will get out the ingredients and we can get them made and drink our coffee while we wait for them to bake.

So how did you sleep last night? Regina felt good after a good night's sleep. The bed was more comfortable than what she was used to sleeping on.

I slept great and what about you?

I think I had the best night's sleep ever. We need a new mattress.

You should get a sleep foam mattress. That is what I have for both of the bedrooms.

Oh, the muffins are done. Let's eat. I am starving.

Me too.

MURDER IN THE NIGHT

It was lunchtime and Regina and Alex both decided to go out to eat and then they would go their separate ways. Regina had things to get done anyway. And to spend time with Rick and tell him about their weekend getaway.

So where do you want to go for lunch?

How about that nice restaurant near the water. It's called The Waters Edge.

Sure that sounds nice. I have been there once but a long time ago.

They both drove separately and met at the restaurant.

When they got to The Waters Edge there were some boats out on the water. Alex always liked to watch them and wished that she could be out there with them. She could picture Max out on the boat and her sitting back enjoying the waves and watching him from behind. He has such a muscular body as he works out when he can. She was glad that he has a hot body to look at.

When they walked in they were greeted by the hostess. Well hello, Table for two.

Yes. Thanks.

They were brought to a table towards the back by a window where they could look out at the water. Alex was happy. She loved being near the water.

So what do you want to drink?

Two glasses of wine, please. Red.

The waitress left and got them their wine and brought it to them. Are you ready to order?

Yes, I am going to have Steak and baked potato with sour cream. Alex was hungry and figured that she would not want dinner after lunch.

And what can I get for you?

I will have the same. Regina said. That sounds so good right now. I have not had a steak in a while.

Ok two orders of steak coming up. The waitress walked away and out in the back of the restaurant.

Well, when I get home I am going to relax. Even though I have things to get done at home, we had fun yesterday. It was a much-needed day for both of us. Besides, we are almost done with our Christmas shopping and to me that is awesome. Because I do not like shopping right before Christmas.

Neither do I. Too many people and the lines are horrible. I might just shop online for the rest of the things that I need.

I did that last year. But Max had to do some shopping at the last minute. But we did it. Like late at night when the stores were not that busy. But I also scored some gift cards that I had forgotten to get. I still have to shop for him. What do you get a guy that has everything?

Does he have a wife?

No. Not even a girlfriend.

Then you get him a wife. Smiles and gets in her car and drives away.

Alex thought about that for a moment. She wants to be his wife.

Alex pulled into her driveway and parked the car. She got out and went in. She was tired and just wanted to relax and read. Grabbing a Soda out of the refrigerator she grabbed her book and sat down. She read into the night until the phone rang.

Hello.

Hi, how was your weekend asked, Max?

It was great. How was yours?

It was good but not as good as yours. I am going to go to bed soon.

Yeah, we booked a place for my friend to stay for a weekend. They both work too many hours and do not spend much time together so we booked them a vacation time away. They need this. Otherwise, their marriage may not last much longer.

Well you sure know how to fix things, don't you? You always have had a great mind about things.

Well, I will try. I feel that people really need to be together if they are a good match. Besides, I got them together.

You did? How come you did not do a matchmaker business instead? Max chuckled.

Well because that is why there are dating sites, and I like an adventure.

So do I. I guess that is why we work well together.

MURDER IN THE NIGHT

Yes, I agree. I really like working with you. More ways than one Alex thought.

Well, I like working with you, Alex. Anyways I will see you tomorrow. Sweet dreams.

You too said, Alex.

Alex got up and went into the bedroom. She read more of her book until she fell asleep.

Chapter Thirteen

Monday Morning Alex had arrived first. Usually, Max was here already. She got out of the car and unlocked the door. She brought coffee for Max and put it on his desk and then went into her office. She checked the messages on the phone and there was one from Robert. He said that he was with family when she called and that he would call her back Monday afternoon.

A half an hour later Max came in and went to his office. He went through the file of the two cases. Something just did not make sense. Lisa or Amy, there really was no reason for it.

Alex walked into Max's office and sat down. Well, Robert called and said he would call back this afternoon. Have not heard from Larry yet. So hopefully he will come in this morning. So what time is Madison coming in?

She should be here soon. Did she not leave a message?

No. Well, hopefully, she shows up.

The door opened and Madison walked in. Sorry I am late. There is an accident down the road. Nothing bad, just a minor one.

Well, I hope everyone is ok, replied Max.

Madison went to her desk and sat down. The phone rang and she answered it. Ok. Can I put you on hold for a minute? She asked the person on the phone. Ok, thank you. There is a Larry on the phone asking for either of you.

Thanks, replied Alex. I will take the call in my office.

By that afternoon Max and Alex went to the diner to eat and then came back to talk to Robert who called and said that he would be in to talk to them.

Robert was there and waiting when they both got back.

So have you heard anything new? Asked Robert.

No, not really. Just wanted to know if you have heard anything? What have you been doing? I know that you were to leave to go to your new job.

Yeah well, that is not happening now because I have been here and they gave the job to someone else.

Oh sorry to hear that, replied Max.

Yeah, I am too because that was a really good job and they could not hold it for me any longer. And I do not have another job. I have asked for my old job back but they filled that. Thankfully I am able to keep my house for now so I have to find another job.

Well thanks for being here to help us, said Alex. She felt bad for him because he got stuck in the middle of all of this. She still believes that he is innocent.

Can you think of anything else that we may need to know?

No, I do not know anything else. Everything I know I already told you. And I had nothing to do with it. I would never hurt Lisa and why would I want to hurt Amy. I didn't even know her.

Ok well please if you find out anything you know from word of mouth or anything please let us know.

I will so can I please go and not be bothered anymore?

We will see. You're not able to leave yet.

Well, I can't leave now. I have no place to go.

I truly am sorry Robert. Hopefully, there will be another job like you wanted to come available for you. You're able to go now. Try to have a great rest of your day.

Thanks. Replied Robert and he left.

Well, I really do not think that he killed either one of them. He really does not have a motive. Alex knew that she had to be right.

The only thing we have to go on is Larry. He has been acting really strange. We really do not have anything else to go on. Max really did not think that Larry could do it or even figure out why she would do it. Well, I think it is time to find out what Larry is really up to.

MURDER IN THE NIGHT

Alex and Max went by the shop to see what was going on. There was a big going out of business sale sign on the front window, and the shop was busy. They both got out of the car and went inside. Larry was out on the floor at the sales register.

Wow, busy day huh?

Yeah, it is. I have to sell the shop. We just are not getting the business like we were. Lisa was the brains of the business.

Well, that is too bad.

Yeah, it is. This is what she wanted and now it's gone. Only fifteen years going and now it has just become nothing. But everything is almost sold. I will sell the shop and move on. We have to have money for her burial. It cost us more than what we expected. We have not even thought about burial plots or anything because we figured we would bury our parents first. I guess more people should think about burial when they are at a certain age.

Many people plan when they are married. I do not have mine yet. Look, we never know when our time is up. Children die as well and it's even harder for their parents to bury their children. Alex understood where Larry was coming from. She lost a family member at a young age and it was very hard for the family to have to bury their daughter after high school.

Well, I see you're very busy so we will go. Good luck today with your sale. We will be in touch with you soon to keep you updated.

Thank you, replied Larry. Now is a good time to buy something before it's gone.

Alex looked for the dress that she had seen but it was already gone. Well, I am too late for the dress that I wanted. She really had some nice clothes here.

Alex and Max both left the store and headed back to the department. Well, let's see if we have any messages?

Hey, there is a new coffee shop there, let's stop and see what they have.

Ok sure. Wonder if Madison would like something. Give her a call. Max never liked to leave anyone out. The polite thing to do is to call and see if she would like them to bring her back something since she is part of the staff.

73

Oh yeah, great idea. Alex picked up her phone and called the office. Madison answered the phone and Alex asked her what she would like.

Madison was glad to hear from them and thought it was nice that they had asked her if she wanted something. A cup of coffee with cream and sugar that is all. Find out how much I owe you and I will pay you when you get here.

No, coffee is on me Madison. See you in a bit.

At the department Alex and Max walked into the office area, any messages asked Max?

No, not today. But I did get all of the filing done and some paperwork done up for you that you wanted to be done.

Ok great, just leave it on my desk when you're done with it.

It's already there. Thank you for the coffee.

Oh, you are welcome. So glad to have you here in the office area when we are not here to interact with clients and new clients. Sometimes it takes us all day at a crime scene so we are not here and we miss messages.

Oh, not a problem. Just happy to be here to help out as much as I can. I can do all of the paperwork while you're working on your cases if it helps.

Yes, that would help a lot, replied Max.

Also just wanted to let you know that we stopped by the shop and they are going out of business. Larry has it up for sale. Said that they have to use the money to pay for the funeral expenses.

So sad. I drove by there the other day. I have never gone in there because I do not dress up much. I am pretty basic in my clothing. She was so young from what I had seen in the obituary.

Yes, she was. No kids and no husband. Just worked all the time. Alex understood why she was still single because it is hard to have a relationship and work in business as well.

Well once he sells it I wonder what his plans are. He really is not able to go anywhere after because we need him here in case we need him as a suspect. Right now we really do not believe that he is one.

Ok well, I can make a note of that into the computer system and then print it and put it into the file. It just makes it easier to do that than keep writing things down. It is much neater that way for me.

Murder in the Night

I agree. So you can go on your lunch break now if you want to.

No, I already ate. I brought my lunch today. I figured I would be busy today but it's been rather quiet here so far.

It usually is in the mornings. So Max what is in the plan for tomorrow?

Not really sure as we do not really have much to go on. I still can not think that we have anyone else to do with the murders.

A call came in with a tip from a caller that did not want to be identified from Amy's apartment. The caller said that the man that was there the night that Amy was killed had gone back to the apartment and was looking for something. She still could not really see who it was but she knew that it was a man. Then she hung up.

Well, I wonder what they were looking for. Maybe that is what he was there for before when he killed her and she would not tell him where it was. I wonder if it was something illegal? Alex could come up with a number of things but that was the only thing that she could think of. It must be drugs or maybe she had something on someone.

I think we need to go and check it out. Just to see what we can find. I am sure that whatever that they were looking for they probably found it. Let's go.

They both got in the car and drove over to Amy's apartment. They stopped off at the office and asked the superintendent to unlock the door.

Just about everything is gone now. Her family has been cleaning out the apartment.

So whatever that they were looking for is probably gone by now. Let's look just in case. We still might find something.

The superintendent had unlocked her door and let them in. Just lock up when you're done.

Sure thing replied Max. Well, let's get started. You look over there and I will look in this other room.

Max had found a bottle of meds that did not belong to Amy. I wonder if she got this from the killer. It has a man's name on it. A Charles Nichols. Pain medicine.

Well, that could have been something that was for her, he might have just given her a small amount of them or shared them with her. I don't think that it is anything to kill anyone for.

It would be for someone that wanted drugs. People on drugs will do anything for them. They do not care what they do to get it. The bottle was almost empty and was sitting on the counter so maybe.

But why wouldn't they just take the whole bottle? Alex took a picture of the bottle and put it in a bag for the lab. We can check it for prints. Alex put the bag in a paper bag to take with her.

Did you find a computer anywhere? Max was hoping that he could find some kind of information on it or at least a disk drive in it. Computers hold all kinds of information.

I will look in the bedroom and living room. The bed was still there and Alex checked all over the room for it. She even looked under the bed. Nothing. Then she checked the messy bed and found it there.

Ok good, we have a few things to go on. Is there a disk drive in it or a sim card?

Let's find out when we get back to the department. Let me check the desk over here and see what else I can find. Alex pulled out the top drawer and found another disk drive. She took that out and put it in another bag and put it in the paper bag.

They both looked around for more stuff but did not find anything else. They locked up the apartment and left. Dropping the bottle off to the lab. They took the computer back to the department to look at and to see what was on the two disks that they found. The killer must have left in a hurry but if they came back to find what they were looking for the second time why did they not get what it was unless they were scared off. Now that the apartment is being cleaned out by the family they must have given up looking for the item or items.

Well, now we have something to do tomorrow. Alex locked the laptop up in the safe along with the disk and went into Max's office. So now what?

What do you mean?

What do you know about computers?

MURDER IN THE NIGHT

As much as I need to know about them. I have looked into a few computers and found information on them that I needed for a case.

Ok well, that is good. I was not sure just where to start on one of them

I usually just check emails. See what their web history is on it and go from there. I can also bring up bank accounts on them as well. This way I can see if she was depositing money into an account or moving money or even withdrawing large amounts of money. What did you do with it?

I have it locked in the safe.

Ok. It will take some time to go through tomorrow. I hope that we can find out something about it. Maybe there is something that she was blackmailing someone with and that is why she was killed. She was strange. Who knows what it was. Max rubbed his chin and smiled at Alex, so what are you doing tonight?

Oh, I don't know. Why?

Would you like to go out for dinner and a few drinks? I will meet you at your place and then drive you back home.

Sure that sounds very nice. A date? Thought Alex. Could it be that he was asking me out? Maybe they could leave work at work instead of bringing it out to dinner tonight.

Ok then. Go ahead and go home, I will meet you there in an hour. I want to go home first before I pick you up. We have done really well with this case as much as we could do. I think we need some adult time out.

Alex told Madison goodbye and that she could go ahead and leave since they were both leaving for the day. See you tomorrow.

She hurried home and changed into something more comfortable. Alex did not want to dress up too much because what if this was like just two friends going out and not actually a date. She grabbed out a nice shirt and a pair of shorts and put them on. She grabbed a glass of wine to help her get ready for going out with Max. She was overthinking things now and she had to calm down because she really liked Max but she still did not want him to know just how she felt about him.

Max came up and knocked on the door. Alex had just finished her wine and went to the door. Grabbing some money she shoved it into her pocket and walked out. There stood Max looking so good on her porch. Well, are we ready to go? She put her keys in her other pocket and she and Max walked out to his car and he was taking her to a restaurant that was nice with a bar. He knew that they both needed a drink during dinner.

Max opened the door for her and let her get in.

Wow so nice to be waited on now. Thank you.

You're welcome. Nice to have a great partner to work with.

You're right because it's hard to find someone to work with that gets along well together.

Max drove to town and stopped at one of the more expensive restaurants to eat at.

Wow, we are coming here for dinner? Good thing I brought enough money. I have never eaten here before. I feel underdressed.

You look fine. We are not here for fashion, we are here to eat. We both deserve this. It has been a tough case.

You're right it has been. And can we leave work at work and just talk about other things?

We sure can. I don't want to talk about work anyways. I just want to concentrate on the good food and the company.

Alex started to blush.

Why are you blushing? Max giggled.

You sure are sweet on words. Alex looked at the menu to avoid looking at Max.

Order what you want.

What? I can buy my dinner.

No, I am buying so don't argue. Just order what you want.

Ok well, let's see. Take me to a car dealership and I will get my new car.

What?

Just kidding. You said I could order what I want. Alex had to smile and Max laughed. She got him to laugh and that made her happy.

Oh, you had me there for a minute I was like wait what? Where did a car get into the food order? Max laughed again. He liked Alex's personality. That is why he hired her because he needed someone that was funny and

MURDER IN THE NIGHT

did not take things too seriously all the time. She knew when to be serious and when not to be.

The waitress came over to find out what they wanted to drink. Max got a beer on tap and Alex ordered a margarita. They were still trying to figure out what they wanted to eat.

They have really good fish here. As well as pasta if you want that to eat.

Ohhh I like pasta. Of course, I like to eat a lot of stuff.

I am going to have the fish. With baked potato and steamed broccoli. Eating healthy today.

Yes, that does sound good. Maybe I will have the same.

Great. You won't be disappointed. Max was glad to get to go out with someone instead of eating home alone again. Oh, he likes to be alone but not all of the time. He needs someone in his life sometime and he is not getting any younger. He wants to have kids someday. But that someday is a few years down the road once he gets his business going to where it needs to be.

Alex noticed that Max was looking at her. What is on your mind?

Oh, nothing. Just glad that you're here. I like the company. I have a few friends but they are busy with their own families now. And besides, I like hanging out with a beautiful woman.

Well, then why are you with me? Alex did not feel confident about herself and has not felt that way for many years. Not since her breakup with her high school boyfriend. They were supposed to get married until he cheated on her.

Max looked at her with a surprised look on his face wondering why she would say that. Because I think that you're beautiful. And why are you still single?

Well, I don't know about that and it's because I do not have time to date anyone. Oh, I have been asked out but I just haven't found the right guy yet. I want someone that is ready to settle down. These guys that I have gone out with are not. They are just too busy wanting to party or something. They live with friends, well most of them do. Before they know it they will be too old and will not be able to find the right one. My work comes first and then maybe someone else. But they come second.

79

Peggy Hargis

I agree. I love what I do and helping others to find who did something especially murder. I am always relieved when we are able to put the killer of their loved one behind bars. But the judicial system does not keep them in for a long time that they should be.

Ok, now we are talking about work again. We have to stop talking about work. I guess we both are so involved in our job that it just can't be helped. That is why we work so well together because we are determined.

Well ok, so what are you planning on doing for Christmas? Have you started your shopping yet?

Oh yes. Regina and I got most of ours done this past weekend. We had such a great time though and I hope that we can do it again sometime soon. I miss having a girl's day out. I am hoping that she and her husband will slow down and spend more time with her husband though. They do not have kids yet and are not sure if they will ever have any because they love their job too much to want to have any.

What about you? Do you want to have children?

Yes, I do at some point. But not right now. I am too busy with work to even think about kids and I have not found the right guy yet. She could not say that she had found the right guy without embarrassing herself. What if he was not that interested in her. She thought that she was but she really was afraid that she would mess things up.

Well here is your food, the waitress brought over their food and then asked if she could get them anything else.

Yes, one more beer, and what about another margarita?

Sure that would be great. Thank you. Alex needed something to calm her down because she was starting to get anxious again. Well, let's eat. This looks really good.

I am glad that we came here. The food is really good and I think that you will love it too.

Oh did you know that Amy's family is doing a memorial service? That is why there is no funeral. We could go. It's this Thursday.

Sure we can go. I feel bad for the family. I mean yeah she had her problems but she was not a bad person. Or at least I don't think so. How is your fish?

MURDER IN THE NIGHT

It is great. The best that I have ever eaten. We will definitely have to come here to eat again.

Wait till you try their prime rib. It is better than most places. Their chef is one of the top chefs around. He moved here last year and the customers have been coming in more and more which made this restaurant one of the best around.

After dinner, Max drove to the beach and they both went for a walk. It was deserted as the sun had already gone down and it was dusk. It was getting cooler out and Max just wanted to do a walk before going home. We have to walk off our dinner.

It really was a great dinner. Thank you.

You're welcome. Thank you for coming with me.

Thank you for asking me. I had fun. That is why we are great friends. We both like the same thing.

So do you need help again with Christmas shopping?

I was going to ask you to help me again this year, yes and you already have your's almost done so Yes I really do need your help.

Ok, sure I can do that. What about this weekend?

That would be great. Thanks. I have everyone that I had last year so it won't be so bad. I have a few gift cards to get but I can get them when I go out another time. I like to give restaurant gift cards. I should have picked up a few tonight where we were but I can get them at the store too.

Hey, that is a great idea. I want to get some too. For my friend that I was with this past weekend. She and her husband can use that. They mainly eat at home all the time. They need a great date night. I have read that even if you're married, date nights are always good to keep the love alive. Alex was happy to be with Max and that he wanted to spend time with her. She just could not believe that he thought that she was beautiful. There are many more other women out there that were much better looking than she was.

I can see how that would work. It's time together and you have to get out of the house and have fun. Otherwise, it could just complicate things and the marriage could go bad.

Yes, couples have to take time together without the kids to just get to enjoy each other.

So where did you come up with all of this information? Max knew that she was smart as well as beautiful and was glad that she was cautious about her looks. He could see beauty in her that she did not see inside and out. She had the most caring heart that he had ever known and he liked that in a woman.

I learned it from watching my parents. They always knew how to keep the romance alive. When we were growing up they did a lot of things with us and not with each other and then they finally realized that they needed time with each other. My mother told me that their marriage almost ended because they did not spend much time together so when we were older she knew that we could stay home without them while they did things together.

Totally agree with that. Well, let's head back home. We have a day to get through the computer. We really need to get warrants to check out Roberts and Larry's homes as well. Why don't you go in and get those tomorrow?

Sure I can get those before I come to work.

Great. Thank you.

You're welcome.

Chapter Fourteen

Alex drove to the courthouse to get the warrants picked up for Larry and Robert's house. She was sure that Robert had nothing to do with it but she wanted to be sure. For some reason, she trusted him to be innocent. She parked in front of the courthouse and went inside. The security guard at the front had her sign in and asked where she was going, he made her a guest pass and let her go.

She finally made it to the department as she had to wait a while for the warrants to be done. They were very busy with early court cases. Alex had texted Max that she was going to be later than she had thought. When she walked in Max was in his office going through the computer. He had the code for the safe and wanted to get in to check to see what he could find out. He did check her emails. Nothing really showed up there until he looked in the deleted files. There was one from Larry and then a reply email from Amy. She had blackmailed him. She knows who the killer is that killed Lisa. But why would he kill his own sister? Max read both emails and then found out his answer.

We do need to check Larry's house. We should probably do a check on Roberts's house as well so we can take him off the suspect list. Just in case they are in it together.

I really do not think that Robert is guilty. I think he loved Lisa too much to kill her.

Well, let's finish this up, and then we will go and do our warrant to check Larry's house first and his office. Max turned back to the computer to finish up what he was doing. He then picked up the disk drive and put it into the

83

computer. To his amazement, he found pictures on it. Some of Larry right after the murder took place. Amy was in on it. So he must have killed her to keep her quiet. This is what he was in her apartment looking for.

Well, that explains who killed Amy then and why. Because she had evidence.

So our other suspect is dead. Here is another picture of Larry with blood on his shirt and what is that in his hand?

Looks like a knife. She took pictures but how did she manage that without being seen taking them?

Because if you look here she is not in the room. She is standing outside of the room in the shop area and snapped the pictures. She then hid the camera and either left or she went and confronted Larry. That was probably why the light was on that night. It must have been him looking to see if someone was on the sales floor and she had gotten out before he could find her.

What was the email that was from Larry? Alex was wanting to find out what Larry had to say to her now. Max printed out the two emails and gave them to Alex. Once she was done reading them he then put them in the file for evidence as well as printed off the pictures that were from the drive.

Wow, I really can't believe that he would think that he could have something on her. I know that she had something on him and it was a lot of something. So we have our killer but why? Why would Larry kill his own sister? So let's find out where Larry is since we have the warrant to search his house and the shop. And if he is at the shop then we will have to have him close it up for the day.

Alex and Max arrived at the shop and Larry was there, he was in his office. He was surprised to find out that they were there.

Well, how can I help you today? Have you found the killer?

We are here to search your office. And the rest of the place. So you might want to close it up so there is not much talk going on. People will be wondering why you have two detectives looking around.

I can't just close the shop. It's busy.

You can close it and you will. Do you really want people talking?

MURDER IN THE NIGHT

Well no. Ok, give me some time. I will go ahead and put up the closed sign and then send the staff home.

Alex, Go ahead and close the place up. Larry can stay back here where I Can see him. Max had a lot to go through and it might be a long night. They still had to search the house.

Alex went out to close the shop. Told everyone to go home. Confused customers and staff were upset about having to leave. The place would probably be closed up for good. Larry would be brought in to be held without bail for his sister's and Amy's murder. Alex locked the door and turned and went to help Max look around Larry's office. Max was looking at the computer to see if he could find the email that was, he also wanted to see who else he had emailed and to see what others had on him.

Max checked all of Larry's emails sent. There was nothing much to be found. All of the emails that he may have sent to Amy are gone. Well, there is nothing here. We will have to look around the house.

So you have a warrant to look around the house?

Yes, we do. So if you're hiding something now is the chance to give it up now because sooner or later we are going to find it.

Well, I do not see how that is legal. I don't want you going through my house.

We have to. And we are going to. The shop will be shut down until further notice. Let's go.

Alex rode in the back of the car with Larry and Max drove to Larry's house.

What are you looking for at my house?

Emails off of your computer and anything else that we can find. Maybe some pictures.

Well, you won't find anything there either. You can't prove that I killed Lisa! How dare you blame me for her murder.

Oh, I think that we will, replied Max.

Pulling into the driveway of Larry's house they got out and let Larry open the door. I am telling you won't find anything.

Max and Alex went in and looked around. Larry's computer was in his home office and he went in to see what was on it.

85

Alex went into the kitchen to see if she could find a knife to match the one they had seen in the picture. Sure enough, there was one in the drawer. She took it out and put it in a bag for evidence. Blood could be shown on it with a certain light.

Alex, come here for a minute. Larry was pacing back and forth. You are setting me up. You still can not prove that I did it.

Oh, I am sure that I just put an email to Amy about the murder of Lisa's and here is an email from Lisa. She wrote that she was not going to give up the shop or make you a partner. She also stated that she had put everything she had into it. Including a loan that she took out and paid back already. Why would you think that she would make you a partner?

Well after all I do help run the place. I am there just as much as she is. I do the hiring and firing as well as payroll.

She offered you a very important position because she knew that she could trust you. But you showed her your trust by killing her. You did it all wrong because you got caught. And we are also charging you with Amy's murder as well.

How can you accuse me of murdering her? You have no proof.

Oh but we do. We have emails to Amy and from Amy as well as pictures.

Well, she was going to. She tried to blackmail me. I did not kill her either.

So you killed your sister because she would not make you a partner and you killed Amy because she knew too much. Alex, call Sargent Adams and have him come down and arrest Larry. We still have some things to look for. We know you did both murders.

I want my lawyer. He will get me out and sue you both.

Go right ahead, Larry. You won't get anywhere. We have the proof. I am just glad that this case is solved.

You got the wrong guy for Lisa. You need to look at Robert.

Robert was not in the room at the time that Lisa was murdered. You were. You're not getting away with it now. The jury will see right through you.

MURDER IN THE NIGHT

After Larry was taken away to jail Max and Alex continued to look around the house.

Hey here is some duct tape and rope. But nothing that matches our victims. Well, let's check around some more and see what we can find that we can use against him.

Check any papers laying around. He may have written something down on it.

Good idea. Max checked the desk and all the draws and came up with nothing. Well here is his cell phone. I will check his text messages. There has to be something on that. Max looked at the phone and found out that there were a few calls made to Amy the night that she died and a text message telling her that he needed to talk to her and for her to call him. There were no calls back from Amy. Well, at least we know that she did not want to talk to him so that must have made him mad so he went after her to straighten things out.

That does sound like what happened. If I were her I would not want to talk to him either. Actually, I would be afraid of what he might do. He does lose his temper easily which is probably why Lisa did not make him a partner. But if he had actually put money into the company I think that she would have. Instead, he wanted something for nothing. Well, this is all coming together now. Ok, so it looks like we are about done here. Let's go home and we will check Robert's home tomorrow. I will go and let Madison in the morning and then we can leave right after.

Ok, I will see you tomorrow. Now let's go back so I can pick up my car.

Alex got home and was hungry but did not feel like making anything. She looked in the cabinet and found an already prepared meal. She liked these on nights like this. After dinner, she went and took a shower and crawled in bed. She turned on the TV and watched the news. The news reporters had already put in about murder suspects in custody. Well, the news sure does get around fast. Alex called Max to let him know about Larry being on the news. They did not release a name yet because that has not been released by the police. Now everyone can breathe easy knowing that a killer is off of the streets. Alex turned off the TV and went to bed.

87

Chapter Fifteen

The next morning Alex went to the department with coffee for everyone. Max and Madison were already there and Alex walked into the office area and handed everyone their coffee. Well, Max, are you ready to go?

Sure. Madison if any reporters call, take a message. We have to go and talk to Robert again and do a search warrant. Max did not want anyone trying to get information that is not released yet like the name of the suspect.

Wow, a second suspect?

Hopefully not. We are thinking that Larry is the only one, replied Alex.

Ok well be careful and I will see you when you get back.

Ok, see you then. If you need anything give me a call. If they should come in, tell them that there are no comments about the arrest. We do not need this getting out in the open too much. Not until everyone is notified about it.

Alex and Max left and drove over to Robert's home. They knocked on the door and Robert answered and they showed him the search warrant.

Are you kidding?

We have to do a search to fully rule you out. Then you can go on with your life.

Yeah until something else comes up. Why do you suspect me anyways? Don't you have her killer?

Well, we do but we still have to go through the trial. But we are not allowed to say who the suspect is yet until we confirm all the details.

Well, I wish that this was over. I have another job to go to that is waiting on me and I have to get ready to leave again. I would like to be cleared of all of this.

89

I am sure you will, replied Alex who was confident that he was not a suspect.

Max found Robert's laptop and looked up history searches and email. He found nothing. He even checked Robert's phone. Nothing on there either. They looked for a few more hours and came up with nothing.

Everything seems to be in order here, said Max.

Just like I thought. So can I please have my life back?

Sure you can. But we just had to make sure that you were not a suspect. You do not seem like someone that would do something like that. Alex had a liking for Robert. He was well dressed which, do not get me wrong, they can surprise you to being like someone that would. But Alex knew her instincts and that was telling her that he was a good guy. So Alex was glad that they did not find anything to incriminate Robert.

Well Robert I wish you well with your new job. Thank you for making our job easier in not finding anything wrong here. You have proved to be innocent.

At the department, Madison had a message for Max. A local newspaper had wanted information and wanted to come in for an interview. Max called them right back and said absolutely not, it is too early yet. We have to wait till Trial.

All of the information was left with Madison so that she could type it up and file it. It was noontime so Max and Alex decided to go to the diner to eat. Madison came along with us. You do not have to wait here, I will leave the answering machine on. After we get back we can finish up the work and then call it a day.

I for one will be glad when this case is over. We usually always have one murder, once in a while, we have two like this one. Once we had a whole family.

Wow, who would do something like that?

The husband's best friend. He had a thing for the wife but she would not leave him. So he just decided to end it for them all. Some best friend he had. That was the worst one because there were children in the family too.

MURDER IN THE NIGHT

Well ok, let's talk about something else. Let's go and eat. Alex did not want to remember that case and just wanted to go and eat. Now that the case is almost over as they had all of their evidence they could go ahead and wrap up the case.

So what do you want to do this weekend Max?

I don't know. What do you have in mind?

Camping?

Hey, that would be great. The great outdoors, campfire, and peace and quiet. Just us?

Yes, just us. Maybe Madison would like to come out and join us one day.

That would be great. Just let me know where and I will call before I come out.

I know this great little place with a swimming area. Alex had the number as she had camped there several times in a cabin there. She would arrange to get a two-bedroom cabin. The outdoors would be just what they need right now. It is stress relief.

Nice, grilled burgers would be nice to have. I have not been able to grill out for a long time with the place I live at. There is no place to set up a grill.

Oh good, then I have my chef. Chef Max. Alex laughed.

They all got into Max's car and went to the diner. It was starting to cloud up to rain. They have not had much rain in weeks and it has been hot for at least two weeks, well up in the nineties. It was time for a break.

Once at the diner they seated themselves. A waitress came over and gave the specials. Asked what everyone wanted to drink and then left to get their order. Everyone had picked the lunch special as their order for the day. The waitress came back with their drinks and then left to go and put in their order.

Once the food was brought out hardly anyone spoke. Until the news came on. Then everyone was talking about the suspect and who it was. No one could believe that it was Larry.

Hey, they must have talked to the police. Well, I guess now everyone knows who it is. They showed Larry walking into the Jail in handcuffs. I wonder how his parents are doing in all of this.

Why don't we go by and talk to them? I think now the reason why Larry was selling the business is that he was planning on leaving town and going into hiding. He wanted to get as much money as he could out of it by selling everything. Well now the parents will be able to put it up for sale and get the money for the burial and Larry gets nothing.

Madison you can also come with us. This way you can put it in the notes and file it, then we will have to go and finish up the case so we can close it out. We have to type up the paperwork for the judge next week.

Ok. This is good as I can find out just how the cases are done and what goes into a case to close it. The more I learn about it the better I will be at my job.

Exactly said, Max.

At Larry's parents' home, they went up to the door to talk to the parents. They already knew that he was locked up as he called them when he was booked.

We are getting the best lawyer that we can afford. Larry did not do this to his own sister. He loved her. He has always protected her.

Well, we have evidence that he did kill her and he also killed Amy that used to work there as well.

There is no way that he killed either of them. Amy had problems, she had a lot of problems but Larry would not kill her.

Well, that is for the jury to decide. I am so sorry for the loss of your daughter and for what happened to Larry.

They were the only two children that we were able to have. I could not have anymore. I wanted five children altogether. They had a great upbringing and had everything that they ever wanted.

Again I am sorry for what you're going through, replied Alex. She was glad that she was single with no children right now.

Back at the department, there was a message on the answering machine. Surprised it was Larry. He was getting a good lawyer and would be out soon and was going to sue them for all he could get.

Good luck on that, replied Max. We have the information that he is definitely guilty. And I am not worried if he sues us because we are bonded.

MURDER IN THE NIGHT

Ok back to work. Madison started back on what she had to do Max and Alex went to get everything together for Monday. They had to get everything done as they were taking Friday off to go camping. Max was really excited.

Alex called and made reservations at the campground for a cabin and then started work on the case. She knew that they had to get distressed before the trial had started. She had also hoped that Madison would fit into the company like Max and herself.

At the end of the day, everything was done and everything was filed. Paperwork was ready to go to the Judge for Monday. Now it was time to relax. They really did not have to be at the department tomorrow but they did want to make an appearance at the memorial service for Amy. They had only been to see the family after she was found that night to give them the news. Now they would tell them that they have her killer behind bars.

Great job now let's go and get some rest. Next week will be busy with the trial. I hope that the judge will get it in right away.

Ok well, see you tomorrow at the Memorial service. Alex was ready to get home and relax. It was a nice evening to just sit out on the deck and drink a glass of wine, maybe even a bottle if needed.

Alex arrived home and it was still nice out. The rain had missed them and went around, The sun was starting to go down. She got a bottle of white wine out of the refrigerator and glass and went out on the deck to sit down and enjoy the view. Off in the distance was a small herd of deer. They stood out grazing in the grass. They must have been out there for thirty minutes before walking into the woods. The birds were chirping nearby in the trees. She loved it out in the country as it was very peaceful.

The phone rang, it was her mom. Hello. How are you?

We are great. Getting ready to leave for our trip.

Oh, that is right. Have fun. We are closing on our case. The suspect is in custody.

That is good news. I bet you're relieved.

I am. Max and I are going to rent a cabin and go camping this weekend.

Seems like you two do a lot of stuff together.

That is what friends do. He has no one really and his parents went back to South Korea for a visit. He wants to go back but he really does not have the time right now. So he is going to wait.

Where are you going to camp at?

New Haven Lodge is about an hour away. Nice and quiet weekend. When I called they had a lot of cabins open. We really need to relax this weekend.

That is good. Go and enjoy yourself.

I will. Madison, our new receptionist may come up for the day. That way it is not only the two of us alone up there.

But isn't that what you want? I know you like Max.

I know mom but I don't want to ruin our friendship. So I just like to be close friends. It is better this way.

Well, you don't know that it won't work out unless you try it.

Mom in all due time if it is meant to be it will be. I just do not want to rush things.

I understand hon but you have been alone for a long time.

And I don't mind being alone. I like my privacy right now. I am too busy to be in a relationship. And working with Max is good enough. We go out and do things together as friends.

That is what you need is friends too. So it is good that you have Max to do things with.

Yes, that is why we plan things to do together and I think we may even plan a trip to South Korea where Max is from to visit. But that will be a few years later.

Well, we are leaving to go on our trip in a few days so I wanted to call and see how you're doing. I will call you when I get back. I just hope that we have a great time.

I hope you have a great time too. You need this. I need this camping trip. Anyways I will talk to you later. Have fun. I love you.

We love you too.

Chapter Sixteen

It is Thursday Morning and Alex got up and dressed up for the memorial for Amy. She then had breakfast and then drove to the church where it was held. Max was not there yet so she waited in her car for him to show. She turned on the radio to listen to music. The forecast had called for mostly cloudy in the high of eighty-five. The sun was out and bright.

Max parked in the parking lot and saw Alex's car. He got out of the car and walked over to Alex's window and tapped on it.

Alex jumped and looked to see Max staring at the window. Oh my, you scared me. She took the keys out of the ignition and got out of the car, locking it before going into the Church.

Max and Alex walked in and sat in the back. Madison was not there yet and the Church was filling up with family and friends. The service was about to start. Maybe Madison changed her mind or had something else to do. Alex had to get stuff packed up for her trip tomorrow or at least get things ready to go. She was excited to be able to spend time out away from everything.

Madison had just walked in the door and saw Max and Alex and sat down next to Alex.

Sorry I am late. Someone called just as I was leaving.

It's ok, it just started.

Wow, there are a lot of people here.

Yeah, there is. Alex was glad to see so many people there as everyone should have people come to their funeral or memorials. It is just out of respect.

I agree. Everyone should be able to have a crowd of loved ones around. Madison had hoped that everyone would be there for her.

The service had ended and everyone was invited to the dining hall for food. Alex and Max decided to stay for a bit and then leave. They wanted to see who would show up. Madison came in and sat down across from Max and Alex. They checked around, really did not have many people there as many had already left. But the few that were left just sat at other tables. Alex went up to get some food for them and went back and sat down next to Max. For those that ate they talked a little bit to the parents and then left. After everyone had left Max and Alex went up to the parents and gave them their condolences again and left.

Alex went home after and started to pack for the camping trip. She was excited to go but this time it was with Max. He has never been there and she hoped that he would have fun. They would get groceries when they got up there. She also packed her bathing suit. She would also get some bug spray for when they were outside at night. After packing she called Max to make sure he had everything for the trip.

Hi Alex. I was just packing stuff up for the trip and getting some laundry done, I have some shorts in there that I want to bring with me.

Do you have a pair of swim shorts because there is a place to go swimming?

Oh good, I was wondering about that. Yes, I will pack them too. Am I picking you up tomorrow or am I riding with you?

You can ride with me. I know an easier way to get there. We will get groceries after we get there. There is a store at the campground.

That would be great. I really do not want to bring a lot of stuff with me when we can get it there. Oh and we can make Smores.

Yes for sure. That would be great. I love that kind of stuff. There is also a place to make a campfire. No TV or anything so I am prepared to just hang out. That is what camping is all about. To just get away. And we do not talk about the case.

Ok got it. Will bring my phone and charger but will not be on it to make calls and I do not want to be bothered with other calls either. It is a weekend to relax and have fun

MURDER IN THE NIGHT

Exactly. Ok, see you tomorrow. Call me when you're ready to go or just come on over. No rush.

Chapter Seventeen

Friday morning Alex got up early and finished all of her things packed and ready to go. She started to load up the car when her phone rang. It was Max

Hello Max. Are you on your way?

Yes, I just wanted to make sure that I was not coming over too early.

No, you're right on time. I am loading up the car now.

Great, see you soon.

Alex was getting more excited now that they were getting ready to leave soon. She has not been there since last year. She had gone up alone and had a great time. More people were there and she just relaxed and was able to get so much stress off of her mind. She had to finish getting everything in the car and go through her list to make sure that she had everything. The cabin was furnished with everything they needed for the kitchen as well as linen for the beds. The campground had taken care of all of that stuff.

Max's car pulled into the driveway and parked next to hers. He got out and put his stuff in the car. Do you have anything else that needs to be packed into the car? Max asked.

Nope, everything is already in it. I even packed some snacks so we do not have to buy that when we get there.

Great idea.

Let me lock up and we will go. Thanks for going with me. We will have so much fun.

That is what I need. I do not get to do many fun things like this and it is always fun to do things with someone else.

Yes, it is. Ok, let's go. Both Alex and Max got into the car. Alex had texted Madison the address to the cabin if she wanted to come out. She really wanted it to be just the two of them but having someone else there makes things less awkward. After all, they were just friends but she liked him more than just a friend. They would have to share a bathroom together. Well, that would be interesting as well. She has not shared a bathroom with anyone since she moved out of her parents' home.

Max got comfortable in his seat and just relaxed while Alex drove out to the city limits and onto the highway. He could not wait to get there and just relax. To be able to sleep in and not have to be somewhere. Traffic was not bad as it was a workday for most people so they were able to make good time.

And here is the campground. We will stop at the store first and they have a little diner where they even serve breakfast. They needed to get supplies. They both got out of the car and walked into the store. There were a few people doing some shopping.

She picked up a half-gallon of milk as they were only going to be there for a few days. She did not want to get more than what they would eat or drink.

Max looked in the meat section and grabbed some steaks. What else do you want to eat?

Eggs and bacon or do you want sausage? Alex always loved breakfast in the morning. I brought some coffee and sugar so we do not need that. Get what you want.

I like both for breakfast. I love your cooking but I like to cook too.

Oh good, I was hoping that you would do some cooking too. I have not had much of your cooking. She grinned at him.

I would love to cook for a beautiful woman.

Well, I will take you up on that. What else are we going to get? What do you want to go with the Steaks?

Baked potatoes. We can grill them on the grill with some butter.

They finished up their shopping and checked out. Alex got the key from the attendant and they loaded up the car with their stuff and then she drove up to the cabin. The front porch had a few chairs so that they could sit out and drink coffee. A few people were outside a few cabins down, the children

MURDER IN THE NIGHT

were playing and ran down to the creek. Max and Alex unloaded the car and then went out and around to check out the rest of the cabin.

So which room do you want Mr. Max? Since it is your first time you get to pick the bedroom. Max looked around and said well what about that one over there.

Ok so we will go ahead and put our luggage in our rooms and then we can go outside and check out on the back deck. Got to find out about the grill. Alex took her luggage to her room and opened the window to let in the fresh air. How do you like your room Max?

It is really nice. The bed is all made up and everything. The bed is comfortable.

She was already getting hungry for lunch. They had picked up some lunch meat for lunch and some chips. They have a full kitchen but why heat up the kitchen when you have a grill. She finished putting the groceries away and then they went outside.

Max was sitting out on the deck enjoying the wooded area. Hopefully, we get to see other wildlife out here. I do not see much in the city.

Well, you're going to love it here then. It was nice to find someone that liked to do the same thing as she did. Hopefully, they have more in common. Alex went out and sat down with Max. Hey, do you want a drink? And maybe a sandwich, we can sit and eat out here.

That sounds like a great idea. Enjoy the great outdoors. Max was getting into being out here. He really liked being outdoors. And he liked to be with her.

Ok, I will go in and make us a few sandwiches and will bring you out a drink.

Thank you. Don't be waiting on me all weekend. I can help out too.

Oh, I don't mind. Trust me I like doing it. Especially when it is like a party. I like to be a hostess.

Well, a man can do things as well. I am not like most men who sit around and let the woman wait on me hand and foot.

That is good. All the men that I have met were kind of like that, but not as bad. I do not mind but when it becomes a habit then that is where I draw the line. Be right back.

Alex went in and made a few sandwiches and brought out some snack-size chip bags and drinks. They ate and listened to the kids playing nearby. That could be me one day. I love children but with my work right now I do not want any. I want to be able to have time for them.

I understand that too. Same with me. But hopefully, we can hire a few more people to partner up with us, and then we won't be working so much.

Wait, we are talking about work again. We have to change the subject

It started out talking about kids. Everything seems to lead up to work eventually.

I know, Alex frowned because she really did not want to talk about work. But it is so hard when you're having a mini-vacation with your partner. How do you not talk about work?

After lunch do you want to go for a walk down to the swimming area so you can see where it is?

Sure, why not. I want to enjoy as much as I can this weekend and I am so happy that we started today. Almost hate going back on Sunday.

How is your sandwich? Alex really was enjoying having Max there. She is learning so much about him.

It really is good. Thank you. You're a great cook. He then smiles at her.

Well, actually I could be a good cook if I actually cooked it.

They walked into the swimming area and there were several kids splashing around and having fun. Parents were standing around in a group talking. There was a volleyball net up and a few teens were playing together there. Not really enough of them to have two full teams. But they were having fun, that is all that matters.

Hey, there is a trail over there. Would you like to go for a walk? Alex has walked the trail almost every time that she comes out here and it relaxed her to be out to see nature.

Sure that would be fun.

Ok, let's go. When we get back we can relax with some iced tea. I have some making in the Sun tea container.

I like tea. Is it sweet or unsweetened tea?

Sweet. I know you do not need the sugar because you're already sweet.

MURDER IN THE NIGHT

But not as sweet as you. No one can be as sweet as you. You have a great personality, are great to work with, and are a great friend. I feel like I can talk to you about anything. You're different than any of my male friends. Anyways this is a great idea to take a walk and then we can sit outside and enjoy the sunshine and maybe take a nap.

A nap? What do you mean by a nap? You're too young to take a nap.

Yes, a nap. I am going to enjoy and relax this weekend. What else would you like to do?

There is a nice little place to go wine tasting down the road.

Um sounds great. I like your way of thinking. A gift shop, I can buy some Christmas items there too.

Oh yeah, I did not think about that. I can pick something up for my sister there. I really like male friends more than female friends.

Why? Max was feeling good about the whole trip now. He felt that he could be himself. He was comfortable around Alex.

I do not have many male friends but they do not judge me much about the things that I do or say. They do not talk about me behind my back. They are pretty cool. They do not like drama.

True. I hate people who cause drama. I had friends in school that all that they would do is hang out and cause drama. It only hurt people in the end.

I have been hurt a few times. I have learned not to talk to my friends as much as I used to about things that bother me and I just keep it all to myself.

That is the way you have to be sometimes. Anyways, let's finish this trail and go to the winery. Hey, look over there. What is that? Max was really enjoying looking at the different flowers and things.

Looks like a bee's nest up in the tree. Hopefully, it is an old nest. Alex was sure it was an old nest as it looked weathered.

It looks like it. And I do not see any bees in it but they could be asleep. And I do not want to be around much longer to find out. I am allergic to bees.

Ok, let's keep moving. Otherwise, we are never going to make it to the winery.

Why do people litter on the trail? They really need to take their garbage with them. They have garbage cans on the trail. Max picked up the empty can and threw it in the garbage. Probably kids. Parents really need to keep an eye on them to make sure that they do not litter.

I would never let my kids just throw things down. I was not raised that way and I will not let my own kids do that. No matter what age they are.

At the winery, it was a little busy. So many great wines to look at. The store had many different wine-related items. Alex picked up a beautiful bottle stopper that had a couple of red roses on it. My sister will love this. She loves drinking wine and she loves Roses. Oh and here is some fudge. Let's get some and take it back to the cabin. This can be our treat for the night.

You're really into this gift-buying thing aren't you and wine.

Yes, I am. I want to check out the bottles of wine and see what they have. Oh, here is a peach wine. It is made of white grapes. Nice. I will have to try it. Strawberry fruit wine I will have to get for my sister. It's made from just strawberries. Ok well, I better get out of here before I spend all of my money. What did you find?

I picked up a bottle of Cranberry wine. I like it with cranberries.

Nice. I do too. But I wanted to get something different. Well if you want we can open the peach one tonight and tomorrow night.

Oh yeah. I would like to try it as well and see if I like it. Usually, I drink beer but I do like wine too.

Ok great. Let's check out and go so I can get this chilling for tonight. So are you having fun so far?

Yes, I am. Very much so. Thank you so much for inviting me to come with you. I am glad that I came.

You're welcome. I am glad that you came. It's a great way to get to know each other better.

I couldn't agree more.

They both checked out and headed back to the campgrounds to their cabin. The kids had left the swimming area. Alex and Max just wanted to sit and relax and enjoy the peace and quiet.

Well do you want a soda and sit outside or bottled water?

Murder in the Night

Water would be good. Thanks.

You're welcome. Alex walked inside and grabbed two bottles of water out of the refrigerator and walked back out on the deck. Children could be heard playing outside and having fun. Perfect vacation time. Alex handed Max the water and then sat down. So now we wait until dinner. What time do you want to eat?

I don't know. Kinda getting hungry now. We can go in and get the food ready but first I should light the grill so it can get hot. It won't take long to get the food ready.

Ok. I can't believe that it is five already. It seems like we just got here.

I know. The time just flies by so fast. I am not ready for this day to be close to over.

Alex got up and went into the house and took out the Steak and grabbed a few potatoes and seasoned the steaks and washed the potatoes before putting them in foil with butter and wrapping them. Max started the grill and then came inside to help but everything was already done.

I would have helped.

You did, you got the grill going. Now we can put these on the grill when it is ready and then the potatoes. We probably should have gotten some Corn on the cob and put that on the grill.

Yeah, we could but I am fine with just what we got. Oh, we should have gotten some sour cream too. Oh well. It will be a great dinner. At least I am not eating alone.

Same. I love sour cream. I don't know why I did not think to grab some. Oh well. Another time.

Max went back out to check on the grill. Alex brought the food out and sat it down on the picnic table. The grill was about ready to cook the food.

After dinner, they sat out on the two chairs on the deck and rested. The food turned out great. Max was happy with a full stomach. You know a way to a man's heart is through his stomach Max said.

That is true. I like cooking for two. Don't forget we have fudge for later.

But with wine? Usually, cheese goes with wine.

Oh, but we do have some cheese. I picked some up at the store. I am going to go ahead and open the wine now. And cut up some cheese to go with it.

Ok. Do you want some help?

Nope. I got it. Just relax.

You know you are spoiling me. Alex was really showing a side of her that he appreciated. She really was a great woman. He needs someone like her in his life.

I don't mind spoiling you. And I just enjoy waiting on other people. Especially those that I like to spend time with. We are great together. Work and outside of work. I enjoy spending time with you. You are a lot of fun.

And you are a lot of fun too. I am glad to spend time doing things together with someone. I have never been camping and this is actually fun. The kids are having fun nearby and I like to hear them.

Well, one day hopefully you will have children of your own. You would be a great dad.

Thank you. Max smiled and blushed almost at the same time. He would make a great dad as Max loved kids.

Alex went in and grabbed two glasses and poured wine in them and then took out the chunk of cheese and started to open it up when Max came in. I have to use the bathroom then I will help you bring out the stuff.

Ok, thanks. That will be great.

Alex was able to get everything done by the time that Max came back out and he took the tray of cheese while Alex took out the wine glasses.

So how long have you been coming out here? Max was very interested in the camping lifestyle.

A few years now. I came here to relax. Not many people camp in the cabins, they mainly do the tents and RV's. I like it over here for more privacy and I can think.

After a few hours of talking, they decided to go to bed.

Chapter Eighteen

The next morning Alex got up and made a pot of coffee and went outside to sit. The air was brisk and cool still. Everyone was still asleep. Alex loved the quietness of the mornings because it gave her time to destress her mind. The cabins helped her renew herself and sometimes she came out a few times a year. She then went in to make herself a cup of coffee and grabbed a book and went out to read. She was glad to finally be out in the fresh air to get back to herself again.

About an hour later Max got up. Boy, I have not slept like this in a long time. Being out here really gets you going and loosens you up. It really feels great to be outdoors. So much better than the city. Maybe I will look for a house in the country.

You will love it. I love it where I am right now. No one is around to bother you. No one to check to see what you're doing. I love privacy.

So why do you come out to the campground to stay here? Max would love to be somewhere that was quiet all the time.

Because it is somewhat different. I used to go camping when i was a kid and I loved it.

Oh, I get it now. I never got to go camping when I was growing up. My parents were not into all of that stuff. I guess maybe it was because there really were not many places to go when they were younger. It really is nice out here and I am enjoying it so much.

They sat and watched the squirrels run around in the trees. A nice breeze came through which felt good. The smell of bacon was in the air. Children could be heard as they were getting up out of bed.

So what do you want to do today? Max asked.

I don't know. Let's see what the day brings us. I wonder if they have events planned for today in the field nearby. Sometimes they do a big cook out there and then everyone brings something to contribute to the dinner. Like a dish to pass. It's a lot of fun. Until some people get a little drunk and act like an ass.

Oh yeah, I guess I can see that happening when everyone is out having fun.

Yeah, it does. That is why we are here to have fun. I have met a lot of nice people here. Anyways, are you ready for breakfast?

Sure am. Dinner was great last night so I can't wait to eat breakfast and see what the rest of the day will be like.

Ok, I will go in and make us breakfast. You want cheese on your eggs or no cheese.

Definitely cheese, please.

Ok great because that is how I like mine too. Oh, I just remembered there is a horse ranch not far from here. We can go horseback riding.

Now that would be cool. I have not been on a horse in a long time. Our day sounds great already. Thank you so much for inviting me out here. You are a lot of fun.

You're welcome. I like spending time with someone else besides just me. And I have gone to the horse ranch a few times to go riding. A group of us go out at a time. We ride for about a half-hour or so. I usually take the half-hour because I get off and I am walking funny after. Not used to being a horse. But it is so much fun.

Ok, I will get a shower now while you make breakfast so that after breakfast you can get a shower, and then we can go to the horse ranch.

Ok sure, Can't wait.

Max was having the time of his life. He has not had this much fun with someone in such a long time.

At the horse Ranch, Max and Alex got out of the car. There were several horses out in the pasture grazing in the grass. A few others were already saddled up and ready to go with riders. They both walked up to the barn and saw a man haltering up a horse to go out.

Murder in the Night

Hello. Are you the man we talk to about the trail ride?

No, that would be Sam. He went up to the house, he will be back in a bit.

Oh ok. How much is it to ride?

Twenty-five for a forty-five-minute ride.

Oh great. Alex took out fifty dollars and waited for Sam to come back. They went out to look at the horses that were tied up for the trail ride.

A tall man came out of the house and walked towards them. Hi, my name is Sam. Are you here to ride today?

Yes, we are. Alex was anxious for Max to get to ride with her. Someone that liked doing the same things that she liked doing. They were so compatible together.

Ok, that will be twenty-five each.

Sure. Here is the money.

Max reached in his pocket to pay his share.

I already got it. My treat. Thank you for coming with me today.

Well here take this and you're welcome.

No, I got it already. Just enjoy.

Ok well, let's get you up on your horses. They are all really great with anyone that is not experienced.

Oh great. I do not get to ride much but I have been here a few times and I always had fun each time.

Sam took one of the horses and brought him over to the steps, Max went ahead and went up on the steps and got up on the horse. Your horse's name is Chestnut.

Don't worry he won't go anywhere, not until mine leaves and he follows.

Sam grabbed the other horse and brought her over to the steps for Alex. You will be on Sally. Alex got up on the horse and took the reins. She put her feet in the stirrups and walked her away from the steps over towards Max. Then Sam got on Magic and he sat there for a bit, explaining about the trail that they will be on, gave a few instructions, and then went towards the gate and opened it up and they went through it. They took the northern trail that was about forty-five minutes long and an easy trail. Max really was enjoying the ride, his horse was pretty laid back and easy going. Alex followed behind Max to make sure that he was ok. When they were on flat land she rode beside him. He really looked good on a horse. He was just as handsome from behind as he was face to face. His black hair shined in the sunlight. Sam stopped up ahead and turned his horse sideways so he could talk to them both for a minute. Now we are going to go down the trail near the creek, the horses can stop and get a drink then we can start back on the trail again. They will just drop their heads down so you will have to loosen up your grip a little and let them drink. I will show you so you will know how to do They started off again and went to the other side of the field where the trail started to slope down a little and then they saw the creek up ahead, The horses stopped for a bit and Sam showed them how to hold the reins so that the horse could get a drink, the horses moved down towards the creek and moved their heads down so that they could get a drink. It was hot and they were thirsty. After about five minutes Sam got them all moving again. They crossed across the creek in a shallow area and went into another field and back up the other way.

Soon they could see the farm again where they started from. It felt like that they had just started the ride. But they both had fun. Sam showed them both how to get off of the horse and Max got off and was walking funny.

Yeah, I have not ridden in quite some time. Who knew how much fun this was. They walked around the barn to look at the horses that were still in their stalls. They were all being let out in certain areas on the farm.

Alex was extremely happy about the weekend. Everything has been going perfectly. Tomorrow would be their last day when they would have to go back to the real world.

They both thanked Sam for the ride and got in the car. On their way back they came across a market stand and stopped to see what they had. Alex picked up a small watermelon and put it in the back seat. The price was great and she could not resist. They had two days to eat it so it was no problem getting a small one.

Once back to the cabin Alex had washed and cut up the watermelon to go with lunch. Alex made a few sandwiches and they sat at the dining

MURDER IN THE NIGHT

room table. It was pretty quiet. The kids were not outside or they may have gone somewhere for the day. There was a water park over in the next county. After lunch, Alex and Max went out on the back deck and sat in the chairs and just enjoyed the fresh air.

We sure have been having fun. Thank you again for inviting me. I would have just been sitting at home. Have you heard from Madison?

No, not at all. Maybe she got busy. And it is an hour's drive out here. She really wanted Max all to herself for the weekend and she was glad that she had not heard from her. She wanted this time away with him. He has been such great company and doing everything that she wanted to do.

They both sat and just looked at the birds and butterflies flying around. Max dozed off and Alex could hear him snore a little. He was so cute when he slept. She could not believe how lucky she was to have him with her for the weekend. He could have said no and she would be there all alone. But she was so used to being alone she really did not mind too much but it would be nice to have someone to share her home with. He did say that he wanted to move out to the country, and she lived in the country and she had a three-bedroom house. He would be a great housemate. But she did not want to ask him and scare him off but then again she could offer him the space upstairs as his own area as she stays in the bedroom downstairs off from the den. She has an office on the other side of the bedroom. She has plenty of space for him to have his area and her space. But then did she really want someone to live with her? It is just a thought for right now.

Max started to wake up. He realized that he fell asleep. It was such a beautiful day and he was relaxed. Sorry, Guess the ride today made me tired.

It's ok and yes it usually does. Something that I am not used to doing a lot. At one time I would have liked to have a horse but now I just do not have time.

I know what you mean. Even if I had time I do not think that I would want a horse. Too much to know about them.

It's about time for supper. Do you want to go down to the diner to eat?

Yeah, that would be nice.

They have everything there and their food is good.

111

PEGGY HARGIS

Ok. Let's eat.

At the diner it was busy. Must be everyone else had the same idea tonight.

Wonder what the specials are. Max was hungry and was interested to see what they had.

Alex and Max picked a table and a waitress came over with menus. What can I get you to drink?

Coffee for me please, replied Alex.

I will have the same, said Max.

Two coffees coming up. I will be back to get your order.

Wow, it sure smells good in here. I am starving. Alex looked over the menu and at the specials. Spaghetti and Meatballs. Oh, that really sounds good. I love Italian food.

Max looked at the specials. Meatloaf with mashed potatoes and gravy. Hmmm well, I will get that.

The waitress came over with their coffee. Are you ready to order?

Sure, said Alex. I want Spaghetti and Meatballs.

And for you?

I will have the Meatloaf, mashed potatoes, and gravy. Max picked up his coffee and took a sip.

Ok, will be back in a bit. The waitress picked up the menus and left.

Well, this is a cute diner. I really like the stuffed bear in the corner. Looks real.

Yeah, it was at one time. The owner had gone bear hunting and shot it up in the mountains.

Wow, I would not want to tango with a Bear that big. Max had only seen one bear in his life and that was near a road he was traveling on.

Their meal came and they ate in peace. It was too good and they were hungry to talk much. Finally, halfway through they started to talk and finished their meal. It was good to have someone to eat with and spend time with.

Back at the cabin Alex took the bottle of wine and two glasses and went out to the deck. Max built a fire and they sat by the fire and finished

MURDER IN THE NIGHT

the bottle of wine. They had to go back to work Monday so tomorrow was their last day. They wanted to stay another day but they both knew that they had to close out the case. It has been a long day said, Alex.

Yes, it has. A long fun day. What are we going to do tomorrow?

We should go down to the swimming area and go for a swim. Then we can dry our clothes before packing them up to go back home.

That sounds like fun. I have really had fun this weekend. It has been the most fun we have had in a long time. Max really felt much better after their trip.

Good, I am glad. Now you know the fun of camping.

I want to come back again sometime. Do you go anywhere else camping?

Sometimes but it is too far to go. It takes a day to get to the place so I do not go anymore.

Well, enjoy the wine. This is really good. I will have to pick up another bottle when I come back out again. I just remembered I will have to cut my grass this week. The kid that does my lawn is away so he won't be able to cut it. It's his summer job so I help him out.

But don't you have a riding mower? Max noticed that it was a good size yard, too big to cut with a push mower.

Yes, I do. Todd uses it when he comes to mow.

The fire was nice to have on their last night being there. They really had a great weekend and Max was so glad that he had gone. The case was really tough on him and Alex and they needed to get away from it all. This would be fun to do after each case. But that would be too much to ask so it might just be him going somewhere after a case is done that they both worked so hard at. It really was tough to get through. One of the worst that they have had in quite some time.

The fire finally died out and it was time to go in and go to bed. Tomorrow was another day and a day that they both had to go back home. Alex did not want this weekend to end.

Well, I think it is time for me to go to bed. This day wore me out.

I agree replied Max. It was definitely a great day.

Max made sure that the fire was out.

Both Max and Alex went back into the house and went to bed. They would have to make the most of tomorrow before they had to head back home. It's always nice to get away but then again it is always nice to get back home.

Alex was almost asleep before her head hit the pillow.

Chapter Nineteen

The next morning Alex got up and made a pot of coffee. Then she got in the shower and got dressed. She was not feeling herself. She was not feeling like going down to go swimming. She just wanted to relax. Maybe after she ate something she would feel better. Besides, it had clouded up and looked like rain.

Max came out of the room and yawned, said good morning, and slipped into the bathroom. He was still half asleep. He then came out of the bathroom scratching his head sending his hair all over. He brushed it to one side with his right hand and walked over, grabbed a cup, and poured a cup of coffee. He then walked over next to Alex and sat next to her on the couch. He rubbed his eyes and yawned again trying to wake up.

It looks like it is going to rain.

Yeah, I see that. Probably best we head back home anyways if there is nothing else that you want to do. I had a great time here and I really do not want to leave but I know that we have to.

Same here. We always have fun together. There is never a dull moment around you. I like it.

Yeah me too. I definitely want to come next time you come out again. Remember do not come out here without me or I will have to fire you. He smiled at her. I am only joking but I do really want to come here again.

Well, we will see. Alex was glad that he wanted to come out again and was looking forward to doing it again with him.

Alex cleaned up the kitchen and emptied everything out of the refrigerator that was theirs and packed up the car. They were not really hungry and planned on stopping on the way home at a restaurant that they passed on the way there for Lunch. Alex went back out on the deck to sit and relax. She really wanted to stay another night because she did not want it to end.

Max came out and he had a pair of shorts on. He looked so hot in them. Alex has seen him in shorts before but these made him look really good.

Wow, I like those shorts on you. Then she started to blush because she could not believe that she just said that.

Thanks. I bought them for the trip. Well, are you ready to go?

Sure. Let me lock up and make sure I got everything. We can stop at that gift shop on the way back home too.

That would be great. I still have to pick up something for my parents for Christmas. My mom loves things from Gift shops.

Ok well, let's go. We still have to drop off the key.

They were finally on their way back home. They had done the gift shop and the restaurant and she really did not want to be close to home. That meant that Max would probably leave right after.

Hey, would you like to stop and get some ice cream?

Yeah, that would be great. It's getting hot out. Would you like me to stay for a while at your place when we get back? I have a feeling that you do not want today to end. We can order out later for dinner. Alex really was up to that. She could do laundry while he was there and ordering dinner would be so good for after.

That would be great. But it is up to you. You are more than welcome to stay. My home is your home.

Thanks. You are always there for me. I enjoy spending time with you. You're a lot of fun.

I try to be. And you're a lot of fun too. I am glad that we work together as a team.

Oh, remember ice cream. It's ahead. Max almost forgot about the ice cream place.

MURDER IN THE NIGHT

Ok. You can order what you want. I got this.

Alex pulled into her driveway. There was a package on the front porch. I don't remember ordering anything. Well, I will unlock the door and start unloading the car. Alex went up on the porch, picked up the package and unlocked the door. Max had started to unload the car and bring in things from the camp. He went back out and took out his duffle bag and put it into his car. Alex came back out and grabbed the rest of the stuff out of the car and went back into the house. Max followed her in.

So what is in the package? Max was wondering what she had ordered. Maybe it is something you had ordered for someone for Christmas.

That could be. She did like to do Christmas shopping online. Alex grabbed a knife and cut the tape on the box. She opened it up and seen it was the shirt that she ordered. She took it out and tried it on. Oh, I really like this. It fits perfectly. She showed Max.

Wow, that does look nice on you. Max grinned.

What was that for? Alex had to smile.

I like it. It looks good on you. Max had to tone it down. He was falling for her and he knew that she liked him too but he did not want to overdo it. Do you need help with anything?

No, I got it. Alex put her clothes from her bag into the washer and started it. Then she went and got a glass out to pour wine in it. Do you want a glass of wine?

Sure. Thanks. I remembered I have to get home to do things around the house. So can we do a rain check on dinner?

Yeah, that is fine. Totally understand though. I am tired and glad to be back home. We had a great weekend.

Yes, we did. Alex handed him a glass of wine. Thanks again for coming and I am so glad that you had fun. So what are we going to do now that the case is almost done?

Just wait for the trial and go from there. Larry has already had his arraignment so the trial will be planned after that. He is detained and not able to get out on bond. If he pleads guilty there will be no trial but I do not see that happening.

Alex was alone, she finished off the laundry and put it away. She then went to bed as she was tired after the whole weekend thing. She loved every bit of it but she needed to be able to just relax now. They just had to get through the trial and then onto something else. Another case was solved and she was glad that it did not turn into a cold case like some that they have done before.

Chapter Twenty

Monday morning Alex and Max took over the case file to the courthouse for the Judge to go through for Larry. Now that Larry was in jail until the trial Robert had continued to move forward with his life. He had already moved out of his house and to where his next job led him. Alex was glad that he had nothing to do with it.

Madison had shown up before they left to go see the judge and to talk to him about what had happened to the murder. After they talked they had gone back to the department and just worked on calls that came in that day about the murder. Reporters wanted to know information and they were not able to give any until the trial was over.

Well, let's all go to lunch. They have already done everything that they needed to do for the case and did not have anything else to do. So they did the next best thing, go out and eat. So far the case is over but not until the jury says that he is guilty. If they do not find him guilty then they will have to appeal for another trial. And that will take longer.

Alex had been to a few trials already and knew that the process would take longer unless if the suspect pleads guilty then there will be no trial. But she was sure that Larry would not plead guilty.

They all went to the Italian restaurant down the street. Alex loved Italian food.

They went inside, it was a little busy but they did not care because they were done for the day so there really was not anything else to do. Alex had some things to do after anyways.

A hostess came over and seated them at a table by a window.

Your waitress will be right over.

Ok Thank you.

Madison looked at the menu. Oh so much to choose from. I actually wish we were able to get what was on the dinner menu.

Yeah I know, replied Alex. She also found something on the list that she wanted. Stuffed shells. I love Stuffed shells.

Me too replied Madison.

Will you two stop looking at tonight's menu and focus on lunch? I don't think that it will do you any good. Unless they will go ahead and make it for you now but I really don't think that they will.

The waitress came over and got their drink order.

Alex had to ask, Are we able to order the Stuffed Shells?"

Let me go ask. I really do not think that they have any ready right now but I will see.

Well replied Max, maybe there is a chance that you can order them.

The waitress came out. We really have not done them yet since it is a dinner item. I am sorry. They can only do lunch right now.

Well that is ok. Maybe I will have to get some to go later. I will stop by. So I will have chicken parmesan with angel hair pasta.

I will have the same reply Madison.

Make that three, said Max. It really does sound good.

Ok great, I will put in your order now.

Thanks.

So what are you going to do for the rest of your day? asked Max?

I have some errands that I have to do. It will be good as I can get them all done. Alex was glad that she had the afternoon off.

I am just going to go home, I don't have much to do today said Madison. Thank you again for inviting me out to lunch.

No problem, said Max. Glad to have you along. You are doing well at the office. Thank you for all you do.

You're welcome. I just do not like sitting at home and trying to find something to keep me busy so I like to do office work. It's a pretty easy job. And you both are nice people so I really like what I do.

MURDER IN THE NIGHT

The waitress came back with their drinks. Your food will be out shortly.

Ok well thanks said Max.

You're welcome. Enjoy.

Wow this is really good, said Alex. This was a great choice. I have only eaten here a few other times and never disappointed.

Yes it is really good replied Max

I am very glad that we got this. Madison was happy.

After lunch they all went back to the office, Everyone got out of the car and into their own vehicles to go on their way.

Bye everyone said Alex. Have a great rest of your afternoon.

You as well, replied Max.

Thank you for lunch and the company said Madison.

You're very welcome, said Max.

Alex got in her car and drove to the post office. She had to mail off some bills. Then she went to the pharmacy and then to the store to get groceries. She was getting low on everything.

Alex went home and put everything away. Then she started getting her laundry done. It was nice to have a half a day to come home and get things done that she normally had to do late at night or catch up all day on her day off. Her phone rang, it was Max.

Hello. Alex, this is Max.

Yes. Did you miss me?

Yeah, then he laughed. I just wanted to let you know that the trial is tomorrow. So that was fast. The judge must have decided to go ahead and get everyone together. They had already got people for the jury to come in.

Well that is good. Alex was glad that they did not have to wait long for the trial because sometimes there is a long wait. But the judge must know that he is guilty.

Yes that is what he had said. All of the evidence points to him so they got him. There is no way that he can get away with what he has done.

Ok well I will see you tomorrow then in court.

Sounds good, replied Max and hung up.

Chapter Twenty-One

Larry was brought into the courtroom and brought upfront. Alex and Max sat in the courtroom waiting to see what happened. Hoping that the jury would find him guilty.

There sure are a lot of people here. Lisa's parents are sitting over there. They look like they are still in shock that Larry could be the one that killed Lisa and Amy. Amy, I could see why he would be angry but his own sister? Alex moved in her chair to get comfortable. They had been there for half an hour and the chair was very uncomfortable.

Amy's family was sitting on the other side waiting for the trial to start.

Max was glad that it was going to start. They may be in court for a week or two depending on how long it takes the jury to come up with a decision.

The jury came in and all sat down and then the judge came in.

The judge asked Larry what his statement was.

Larry replied I did not mean to kill my sister. We argued and then she threatened to fire me as her HR employee. I still felt that I should have been her partner in the business. But she wanted me to put in half the money and I just did not have that kind of money. So I had to make it as someone else killed her. I am sorry for what I did to her and my family. I wish I could take it back but I can't.

After a while, there was a recess and everyone was able to get a break. The jury had to go in and talk with themselves to see what the verdict was going to be. All of the evidence was clear and Larry was guilty.

PEGGY HARGIS

The jury came back into the courtroom and the judge asked what the verdict was and Juror number one stood up and replied, Guilty in the first-degree to two counts of murder.

Larry was sentenced to thirty years in prison.

The sheriff then walked Larry outside and into the prison van.

Everyone stayed for a bit and was talking amongst themselves, then slowly got up and left.

Alex and Max got up and left to go and close the case file and put it away. Another murder was solved. Neither one could not believe that he was the one that actually did it.

Well, I think we deserve a nice dinner as we have worked hard through this case but still am shocked that Larry did it. I had thought that Amy did it until She ended up dead. Alex walked to Max's car and got in.

I don't believe it either Max said getting into the car and starting it, pulling out to go to the Steakhouse and Ale. A well-deserved dinner is on me, replied Max.

The restaurant was not very busy so they were able to get in and get seated right away.

I really like coming here, said Alex.

What can I get you to start off with?

I would like a glass of red wine, replied Alex.

I will take your specialty beer on tap, said Max.

Ok, any appetizers?

What about the sampler platter please, said Max.

Sure I will get these right in, said the waitress and she walked away.

So what are you going to have? They have so much food on the menu that sounds good to me but I still want a steak to go with it. Besides, we both deserve it, said Max.

Steak and potato are what I want but I do not know if I want a baked potato or if I want a baked sweet potato. I love it with cinnamon sugar and butter.

That sounds good too, said Max. With a side salad and bread. Steak and shrimp also look good. Order what you want I am buying.

MURDER IN THE NIGHT

Their drinks and appetizer came out, they were hungry so they sat quietly eating their food.

Max then said, well what is next? What are you going to do this weekend?

Not really sure. I may go to the beach south from here and stay in a hotel. Just get away for a few days. Want to come with me. I mean not sharing a room but just going and staying in the same hotel. She was hoping that he would say yes so that they could spend a nice weekend away and get to focus on each other and having fun instead of working all of the time.

That sounds like fun. I can use some time away. My neighbors are noisy and moved in next to me so I am really wanting to get away.

Ok great so I will look online tonight and find out where we can stay and call you to see if you are ok with it or not.

No, just reserve two rooms for us both. Whatever you want to stay is ok with me. It gets me away for a while.

Great, I will do that once I get home. We will have fun. I usually find a hotel with a restaurant in it so we do not have to go far to eat if we do not want to leave the hotel.

After dinner, Max dropped Alex off to get her car and then followed her to her place to look online for hotels.

This one looks nice, quiet, and on the beach. Great reviews. Max was happy with their choice. This should be a great weekend. Another great weekend with Alex. Max could not wait after their weekend at the cabin. He knew that he needed this as much as she did. This case was one of the worst that they have seen in a long time. And a shock to learn that a brother who was supposed to love his sister so much that he would murder her.

They both agreed on the hotel and booked it for the following weekend starting on Thursday. They wanted an extra day to relax as they both deserved this trip. They looked to see what there was to do in the area.

Well, we can go whale watching here. That would be fun. There is also a day cruise on the lake that we can do one day.

That sounds like fun Max said. He was getting excited because he has never had someone that was so much fun to be with. Alex liked to have all these adventures, Max liked to go on these adventures with her. But he too was not wanting to rush into anything because he loved their work-life and friendship. Should he risk it all and tell her how he really felt? Could they actually become and remain a couple? He has not been able to be friends with his ex-girlfriends as it was a bitter breakup.

This trip was going to be different as Alex has never been to this new spot before but she had heard about it from friends. She needed this trip. There is nothing better than getting away from it all. And this last case was a bad one. She just wanted to be with Max again doing something fun. But she was not going to tell him that.

Well, I have it booked so let's get some things done so we can enjoy our trip out. We will plan our trip activities as they come. I look forward to seeing you. You can ride with me.

Ok well, I will see you then on Friday morning?

Sure that will work. Can't wait to go on our trip.

Chapter Twenty-Two

Friday morning came and Alex was ready to go. She had already loaded up the car and was waiting for Max to get there. She was excited about going to the beach and hoped to get some rest and see the whales.

The phone rang and it was Max. Hello Max.

I am running late. I woke up late and I am putting everything in the car and will be on my way.

Great. The car is already packed. I will see you when you get here.

Thanks, see you soon.

Ok well, Max was on his way. She was glad that she had already packed the car and now she could rest a bit before he got here.

Alex's phone rang again. It was her mom. Well hello, Mom.

Hi, how are you? We got back last night but did not want to call because we were so tired.

I am great. We finished up the case and I am going to the beach. But she was not sure if she should tell her mom that she is going with her boss. I booked a room on the beach with a balcony. This case has been a bad one. I hope that we do not get another one for quite some time like what we had. It really is emotionally stressful to see something like that happen to a person. So sad.

I understand Alex and I appreciate you for what you do. It takes a special person to do what you do.

Yes, it is very much. But that is why I take trips to get away when I need to.

Well go and enjoy your trip. Ours was great. We met some new friends and we will be in touch with each other soon. You should have seen our room.

127

Oh really. I am glad that you had fun. Send me pictures of the trip.

I will. Thanks. Will talk to you later. Call me when you get back.

I will do that mom. Thanks.

Max pulled into the driveway and hopped out of the car. He was excited about the trip. He grabbed his bag and put it in the trunk of the car. He then locked his car up and got into the car and they were ready to go on the road. Sorry I am late. The traffic was not great either.

That is ok. The only thing that matters now is that we are on our way to freedom.

At the hotel, Alex checked in and they both got their keys to their rooms. Alex could not wait to relax here. They went up to their rooms which were next to each other just the way that Alex had put it up for. They both went into Alex's room and checked it out. Oh, look there is a minibar. I also have a mini-fridge and a microwave.

Alex went into the bathroom. Wow, look at this tub. Awesome. There is a pool and a jacuzzi downstairs. Hopefully, we can enjoy it later tonight that is if you want to go. If not then maybe tomorrow. We have a few days or longer if we want to stay here. We could use a week's vacation.

True. That would be nice. Well, I am going to go to my room and relax for a bit. I will leave you alone. Give me a call later or text me.

Ok sure. See you later.

Max picked up his bag and went out the door leaving Alex alone to get some rest before they decided to maybe go to the beach.

Alex hung up her clothes and turned on the TV. She picked up the brochure with specials on it. There is a beach party for the weekend. How fun would that be with a bonfire? She walked over and looked out the window to the balcony, she opened the sliding glass door and walked out, and sat in the chair there. Many people were out on the beach enjoying the view and the kids in the water. It was fairly warm with a gentle breeze. Birds were flying around singing in the trees. The flowers lined the landscaping area of the grass area which was beautifully laid out.

A door opened on the next balcony. It was Max. He laughed. I figured you would be laying down watching TV for now or something.

Murder in the Night

Nope, I had to come out and see what was going on outside. It's beautiful here.

It sure is. Thank you for letting me come with you. This is going to be great. Did you know that this is a five-star hotel?

Yes, I did. I saw the ratings. It's really clean here and modernized. But we have not seen the rest of the hotel yet. Come on, let's explore. I am too excited to just relax right now.

So am I. Meet you in the hallway.

They both met in the hallway like a couple of kids on Christmas. This is so neat. I am so glad that we found this place. Ok, let's check out the swimming pool area first. They have one inside along with a jacuzzi. I am sure that there are probably families down there.

They got on the elevator and went down to the first floor. They walked by the hotel restaurant and stopped to look in.

Wow, that is really big. They must stay busy here year-round. Well, let's go and check out the pool. Not that we will go in the pool but the jacuzzi I want to check out. We have a beach to go to enjoy later. I want to walk around to see what else is on the beach as well.

This must be the pool area as Alex had grabbed the door and opened it. The smell of chlorine had come out into the hallway. There was no one in the pool, only a couple in the jacuzzi.

Hello. Alex walked over to the couple in the water. We are coming out later here.

That is great. It's really nice and since we have been here it has been quiet here. Most everyone stays on the beach since it is nice. Unless it is raining.

What time is it open till asked Alex?

Ten at night. The lady in the hot tub smiled and said, my name is Alice and my husband's name is Tom.

Oh, nice. My name is Alex and this is my friend Max. We are here on vacation.

Oh well, I think you will enjoy it here. It is very quiet during the daytime. We are up on the top floor so we do not hear anyone that much.

129

I had booked the room in advance and told them I wanted a room with a view but away from everyone. We like our quiet.

Well, I don't blame you there, replied Max. We are here to relax. Although I love children but do not have any myself.

Ahh well, that's ok. You still have time , Alice said.

Where are you from? asked Tom?

North of here. Two-hour drive. We wanted to come here to get some rest. It has been a rough few months.

Oh, what do you do? asked Alice?

We are detectives. We have our own office.

Wow, that is good. But I guess it's stressful too.

Yes, we also have missing persons as well. So we have several cases that we work on at different times. We just closed a case.

Oh is that the case that was just in the paper?

Yes, that is the one, replied Alex. We really can't get into detail on it. Just what was said in the paper.

Well, that was a tough case. I am glad that he is in prison. Alice got up and out of the Jacuzzi. It was nice meeting you. Maybe we will run into you again.

Nice meeting you, said Alex. They turned and left the pool area and checked out the exercise room.

Max was looking at all of the equipment. He was happy that he could come down here and work out. You know I had thought about putting some stuff in my spare room just to work out with and with a TV in the room while I work out. But I am not sure how long I will be there. I am currently looking for another place to live.

They then left the room and went back down the hall and went past the front desk and outside. They were happy to be able to be outside on such a beautiful day. It was 80 degrees out and there was a nice breeze going on. The smell of food drifted by their nose and it smelled good. I think I smell barbecue chicken. Alex looked the way that the smell came from. Oh look, it must be coming from over there.

Max agreed. It does smell good. And we have not eaten since breakfast.

MURDER IN THE NIGHT

Well, I did not have breakfast. I was too excited about coming out here. I am like a kid when it comes to trips like this.

I see that. Well, let's go and get some food. They walked over to the food truck and checked out the menu.

Hmmm, chicken and fries. That sounds good. It's special with a drink.

Two number two specials please said, Max. He put the money upon the window. The man picked it up and gave him back his change. It will be up in a minute.

Thank you, said Max.

Thank you, said Alex to Max.

You're welcome. They sat down at a table and waited for their food.

Well, this is a great place. I think we will have to come back here again. I love it that I have no pets and no responsibility that I can just go when I want when I can to just go and get away from it all.

But your place is out in the middle of nowhere. It's pretty quiet out there.

Yes, but I feel more at ease when I am not at home and just somewhere that I can relax at. Plus I do not have to do any housework. Everything is done for me.

That is true. Max had to think about that and agree. Being single for so long he was used to keeping everything up himself.

Number two special is up called the man behind the food truck. Max got up and got the two meals and brought them over to the table.

Oh, it smells so good, replied Alex. She picked up the chicken and bit into it. Mmmmm it is very good.

Max took a bite of his chicken and agreed. Yes, it is very good. The fries are also good. So maybe we will have to stop in again before we leave.

Yes, I agree if we do not forget. But at least we know to come back when we come back to visit, said Alex.

After lunch, Max and Alex went for a walk on the beach. There were several stores along the beach and most of them were busy. Well, we can check that out sometime later when it is not so busy.

PEGGY HARGIS

Alex spotted a gift shop and it was not as busy as the other stores and she went inside. She found a few items that she could give to family. She always liked to get souvenirs for her family and this was a perfect place to do that.

Oh there you are. I was walking along and did not see you come in here.

Sorry. I saw this cute Christmas ornament and wanted to check it out. I thought you saw me come in.

No. But what a great idea. I can get some of my gifts here as well.

Yeah I like going to gift shops when I am away on vacation and getting a few items for my family. My mother will really like this cute dog ornament. It looks like a dog we once had when we were kids.

Awww that is cute. You had a lab when you were little.

Yes, his name was Smoky because he was black with a grey look in his fur. He was the best dog that we have ever had.

I am getting my father this Football ornament because he likes football.

I don't see much of anything else right now that I would like to get. I do want to look for some shirts for my sister's kids at that shop that we passed earlier. Maybe I can get them all matching shirts.

Yeah that would be cool.

So are you ready to go back to the hotel. I kinda want to take a nap now. It is so beautiful here and I want to see more but after the drive and being out here I think I ate to much at lunch.

Sure that is fine. Maybe I can find something good on TV.

At the room Alex put her items in the suitcase. She did not want to forget anything when she left to go home. She was happy that Max had come out with her but she would have been fine if she came out alone too. She was used to being alone but she really liked Max and he was really starting to open up more to her. Alex decided to lay down and fell asleep. She needed the rest.

Max fell asleep while watching the game and noticed that it was starting to get dark out. He checked his watch and saw that it was almost eight-thirty. There was a missed call on his phone. Alex had called him at Seven. He called her back

MURDER IN THE NIGHT

Hi Alex, Sorry I fell asleep.

That's ok. Do you want to go and get something to eat or just get room service?

We can go down and get something to eat. Hey we are on vacation right? I will meet you in the hall.

Alex hung up and grabbed her debit card and put it in her pocket and went out to the hallway.

There she is. You look all relaxed now.

I feel better since I got some rest. Hopefully we can go down to the pool tomorrow.

We will see. I kinda want to go to the beach if it is not to busy.

Sure, we can do that. Alex was just glad to be able to enjoy herself in the sun.

The restaurant was not too busy since it was late in the evening. They sat down and looked over the menu. They missed the buffet as everything was picked up from it.

Ahhh we missed the buffet. I love to eat a variety of things.

Yeah we did. We will have to see if they have it in the morning too because I love breakfast. Max was kinda sad that they had missed it.

The waitress came over to take their drink order and left.

Well we have the whole place to ourselves now. Everyone had left. Go ahead and order what you want. I will buy it this time.

Ok. And I will get breakfast in the morning.

Deal. Wow the Angel Hair Pasta looks good. I hope that they have some left.

Yes it does. But I think I want a salad. Max closed the Menu and looked around the restaurant. They have all kinds of beach things hanging up on the walls and pictures. Looks like they are the people that stayed here.

Yeah I love that kind of stuff. Just wonder where everyone is from.

The waitress came back with the drinks and took their order.

So they have a bonfire later. Would you want to go to that? Asked Alex.

Yeah that would be fun.

After dinner Alex and Max walked down to the bonfire. There were not many people there. Just all adults. Alex was happy that there really were not many people there, she found a place to sit down by the fire and Max sat down next to her.

A guy came around and asked them if they would like a drink.

Sure. can I get a soda?

Yeah. And what for you?

I will have the same. Thanks.

The guy went to the cooler and pulled out two cans of soda and brought them over to them.

Thank you.

You're welcome. Welcome to the beach party. There are snacks at the table go ahead and help yourself.

No, I am ok. We just ate dinner.

Ok well it's there if you want it anyways.

Wow I wonder if the Hotel supplied the food too.Max opened his soda and took a drink.

Maybe. Alex was too full to think about food.

Anyways, are you having fun so far. I know we have not done much but I really like it here.

Oh I love it here. We are going to have so much fun here. Alex could not wait to do stuff tomorrow. I just want to relax and have fun.

Yeah me too. I mean that is what we are here for right?

Yes definitely.

A band started to play nearby.

Hey some country music. Someone started singing some songs from Alabama.

Cool, I love Alabama. Max had got to love Country music. He also liked other music. But Country had been calming to him.

They were the last ones to leave and said their goodbyes to the band and told them what a great time that they had.

Well this was a great day. Even though we napped through part of it. Tomorrow we will see what is going on.

Yeah that would be good. I need something interesting, replied Max.

MURDER IN THE NIGHT

Walking in the hotel there was a family checking in. They were a young couple.

We just got married.

Well congratulations, said the clerk behind the desk.

Up at the room Max said Goodbye to Alex and went down to his room.

Alex watched him and opened her door and went in before he saw her still standing there. She was having fun. It was hard for her not to say anything to him. She would have had fun even without him because she was used to going alone but being with him made it even more of an adventure.

The room was cool and Alex was ready to get to bed. She changed her clothes and then turned on the TV for a bit to check the news. There was nothing interesting on the news so she turned it over to watch a movie.

Chapter Twenty-Three

The next morning Max sent a text to Alex for her to call him when she got up. He had already gotten a shower and was ready for the day. He turned on the TV to watch and then looked out on the balcony to look out on the beach. There were already people up and out on the beach with their coolers and blankets enjoying the sun. Children were running around making sand castles and swimming. Other people were playing volleyball. This definitely was the best vacation that he has ever been to. Seeing everyone just having a great time. Children running and laughing.

Alex woke up and checked her phone. She saw that she had a new message from Max. She called him.

Hello. I just wanted to tell you to call me when you're ready. I am up and ready. I came back and fell right to sleep.

Wow. Well you fell asleep faster than I did.

Yeah I guess it was the fresh air that relaxed me. Anyways call me when your ready to go

Ok will do. See you in a bit.

Alex picked out her clothes for the day, blue jean shorts and a pink button up top. Took a shower and pulled her hair into a ponytail and then put on some make up. She has not put it on in awhile so she wanted to look nice. Today was going to be a special day.

Alex called Max to let him know that she was ready and then she met him out in the hallway.

Wow you look nice with make up on. Max had never seen her with makeup on. I guess this vacation thing is working. She looked really nice just to go to the beach.

They both walked down to the elevator and went down to the first floor for breakfast. Max paid as promised. After they ate Alex had grabbed a paper to see what was going on. Boat rides. Hey, we can go on a boat ride. Are you in?

Sure I would like that. How much and for how long.

Twenty dollars for an hour ride. The next one leaves in a half hour.

Hey I am in. Let's go.

Alex left a tip and they both headed out the door and out onto the beach. They both looked around and found the boat ramp across the way.

The ticket booth was near the boat ramp and Alex bought two tickets along with two waters for the trip.

I have never been on a boat here in the US. I have been on a few in Korea when I was a kid with my parents. We had fun when we were kids. They still have one that is all lit up at night and you can go on the little cruise, it is so nice. They had it there for years and it is still there. I want to go on it next time I go out there if I get the chance.

I have been on them a few times at camp. And we also were in a canoe. That was fun.

I never got to go to camp when I was a kid. My parents did other things with us when we were kids. We traveled some but not every summer. We went to Japan once, had a great time.

Japan sounds like a nice trip to go on. It's another place I would like to go and visit.

It would be a great trip to go on. But I really want to go and see where you had lived when you were younger. I have looked at videos online about South Korea.

Oh you have huh. Did you find anything that interests you? Max was surprised that Alex knew more about SouthKorea.

Yes, the street food. Always wanted to try street food. All of the videos were starting to pay off on her knowledge.

Here comes the boat. So here we go for an hour tour. I hope that we do not end up shipwrecked like that one TV show.

MURDER IN THE NIGHT

I don't think we will. Here is your ticket. And water. Not sure where we are going to want to sit.

What about up front?

Sure I guess so. Anywhere is fine with me.

Max got on and Alex went on after and they moved to the front of the boat. It was starting to fill up fast with other passengers.

Wow I guess that this is a popular thing to do.

Yeah. At least the seats are comfortable.

Yes.

After everyone was on the boat it went through the tour and around a few islands with homes on them. The captain had narrated where everything was and how the people had to go by boat over the island to their home. It is more retired people that live on the island and everyone on the island has their own boat to get from one side to the other. There are no cars on the island.

After the tour everyone got off and headed to the beach. Max and Alex decided to go and find some food. There was a restaurant that had seafood.

Oh, that sounds good.

Yeah, it does. I want Lobster. Max loves all kinds of seafood. Including fish.

Walking in the place was full, There was one table to the back. They waited to be seated.

A hostess came over and got them seated right away. Everyone was eating and enjoying their meal.

The hostess left them with menus and told them that their waitress would be over to take their order

The waitress came over and got their drink order. And since they already knew what they wanted to eat she took their food order as well.

Wow, it sure smells good in here.

Yes, it does. We may not want to eat supper after or maybe have something light. Hey when is that Whale watching boat ride?

I think about tomorrow. I will have to check. I believe that it is a half-hour drive from here.

The waitress came out with their drinks and shrimp cocktails.

Oh, this looks so good. I can't wait for the lobster to get here.

139

Alex and Max sat quietly eating their shrimp because they were really hungry.

And then the Lobster came out. Baked potato with butter and sour cream on the side. Corn on the cob as well.

Oh, this looks so good. They definitely would not have to eat later.

Wow, there is a lot of food here.

Yes, it is but it is so good.

We can go to the beach later after we walk off this food.

Or maybe we can swim like a lobster, Max was in a good mood today. He was being funny. Much better than his actual work self.

I don't think that we can swim like a lobster. She laughed a little and then went back to eating her lobster.

After dinner, they decided to go for a walk. Just to get some exercise and to digest their food. The walk would do them good and maybe even find something else to do on their walk.

On the beach, many children were playing and swimming with their parents. Many of the women were laying out, getting a tan or reading. A set of kids were burying their father in the sand. More kids were chasing each other around with water guns.

So you want to grab some ice cream? Said Max. There is an ice cream stand over there.

Oh yeah, that would be good. I could use something cold.

They walked over to the ice cream stand and stood in the line.

Hey we can even get sprinkles. They also have dipped cones. Alex looked over the menu to see just what she wanted. Everything looked so good. I will buy the ice cream.

Ok. That sounds good. I never pass up ice cream. Max grinned at Alex. So what do you want to do for supper?

Wait, we finished lunch an hour ago, we are going to eat ice cream. What do you want to think about supper already?

Because I am thinking about a nice steak dinner.

Does your stomach ever get full? I swear you are like a bottomless pit. Alex laughed.

MURDER IN THE NIGHT

Hey, I have a man's stomach. I can eat a kitchen sink and not get full. Max nudged at Alex and smiled.

I understand. I guess I just never ate that much even when growing up. I have to watch my figure.

Your figure is nice. Nothing wrong with it.

Alex blushed, Thank you, Max. That is quite a compliment. I had always thought I could lose a few pounds.

No way. You're perfect. Max winked at her.

Are you flirting with me?

Maybe but also speaking the truth. You are a beautiful woman.

Alex had to look away. She was smiling so much and blushing. She could not let him see that he made her blush. She could not believe that he said that she was beautiful. She just felt like she was average. She did not have much luck with guys. They teased her for being too thin. She was picked on in school and called a toothpick. One boy called her Ethiopian until she threatened to punch him. He left her alone after that. She was not one to make fun of other kids.

Finally, it was their turn to order.

Max ordered a Chocolate chip ice cream cone. Alex ordered the chocolate chip mint dipped in chocolate. They found a table and sat down and enjoyed their cone and talked about the trip so far. They both were enjoying their time together.

Alex decided to go back to her room to relax. Max wanted to check out the shops to do some Christmas shopping.

Alex went out on the balcony to sit and watch the other people out on the beach. The nice breeze was great on what was a hot day. She was glad that she picked this hotel to stay at. It was perfect and near everything. She will definitely have to come back again and make it her place to visit.

Max texted Alex a picture of him standing next to a large fish that was on display in the store. It was stuffed and he had this big grin on his face.

Alex texted him back. Is this your date? I am glad that you're having fun.

Max sent her a smiley face back. Then went back to shopping.

Later that night Max called Alex. What do you want to do for supper tonight?

Well, we can go downstairs to eat. I am not really hungry so I will get something light.

Ok. Are you ready to go? Asked Max

Let me get ready and I will call you back. Replied Alex.

Ok, see you in a bit, replied Max.

Sure. Alex got up and put on some perfume and fixed her hair.

She called Max to let him know that she was ready.

Ok, I will be out in a bit.

Alex grabbed her hotel card and left.

Hi. You smell nice. Is that a new perfume?

No, just something I had before. I like the scent.

Oh. I do too. Would you like to go to the bar after? It's somewhere on the first floor I think near the restaurant.

Sure we can do that.

Ok then.

I am buying dinner by the way. You paid for lunch.

Ok, that is fine.

They went and found a table and sat down. There were a few other people there.

A waitress came over and gave them two menus.

Can I get a coffee with cream and sugar? Alex needed the caffeine. It was still early and she did not want to be tired. She wanted to enjoy the evening.

Sure and what can I get for you?

I will take a Lemonade.

The waitress left with their drink order.

So what are you going to get? Asked Alex.

I still want Steak. I think I am going to have mashed potatoes and gravy with it.

That sounds good too but not for tonight. I think I will get a Taco Salad. I love it.

Hmmm, Mexican food. Nice. Max smiled at Alex. I am having a great

MURDER IN THE NIGHT

time here. Thank you again for asking me to come along. I just do not get the chance to get away much with our work schedule.

Well, I am glad that you came. Mentally you have to destress after a case as we had.

I agree. It does get to me sometimes.

The waitress came back with the drinks. Can I take your order now?

Sure, I will have the steak with mashed potatoes and gravy. It just sounds so good.

And what about you? Asked the Waitress

A taco salad with sour cream thanks, replied Alex.

Ok, coming up. So are you two having fun?

Oh yes very much so. It is really nice here. I love the hotel and the beach is really nice. I love watching the kids playing and having fun.

Well, that is good.

After they ate Alex and Max went to the bar and sat down at a table. What would you like to drink? asked Max?

Draft beer, please.

Ok, be right back. Max went up to the bar and ordered two beers and then came back.

Here you go. One beer for the lady.

Thank you, Max. You are very sweet and fun to be with. I am so glad that we work well together.

Well, I like to take care of my workers. I like to keep them happy.

So far I am your only worker besides Madison.

Well, that is true. I am happy to have you working with me. You are a great partner. You really know the job.

Thank you. It really is hard to find someone that works well with each other.

Max finished his beer and went to get another one. Alex was still sipping on hers.

So what do you want to do tomorrow?

Not really sure replied Alex. We have a few more days here before we have to go back. I am not sure I want to go back. Maybe we can do the whale watching tomorrow. And then we can just hang out at the hotel the day after.

PEGGY HARGIS

That is ok with me. Doing the Whale Watching tomorrow would be nice.

I think it is a two-hour boat tour of where the whales are.

Ok well, we will check it out and see what we need to do and what time that it is so we do not miss it.

Both Alex and Max got up and went back up to their rooms for the night.

Good night Max. Alex was tired from their day.

Good night Alex. They had a great day together. Alex was having a great time but was missing being home. They would be home soon enough and back to work once a new case opened up.

Alex got ready for bed and turned on the TV to watch the news and then turned it over to a movie. She actually was able to stay awake through the whole thing. Then she turned it off and went to bed.

Chapter Twenty-Four

By morning Alex had woken up around 9 am. Guess she was tired, she thought. She usually never sleeps that late. She got up, got a shower and got dressed. Then she checked her phone again to see if she had received any missed calls. None. Hmmm must be Max slept in as well. She walked out to the balcony and it was sunny out and a breeze flowing through. It felt good. Max had his sliding glass door open and Alex could hear the TV on. She decided to call Max.

Max heard his phone going off as he was stepping out of the shower. He rushed to grab it but Alex had already hung up. He called her right back.

Alex heard her phone ring and she saw that it was Max. Well hello there sleepy head did we oversleep.

No, I was awake by eight-thirty. What time did you wake up?

Oh not till nine.

I am not the sleepyhead then. Max smiled. What time do you want to go down to get breakfast?

Well I am already ready. Replied Alex.

Oh ok well I just have to get dressed. I just got out of the shower.

Alex was picturing him all wet and no clothes on. She smiled but had to not let it show. She did not want him to know what she was just thinking. Ok well just come on over when you get ready.

Sure thing. See you soon.

Now she could not get the picture of him being wet and in the nude out of her mind. Which was fine for now but not for long because she had to stop thinking like that.

PEGGY HARGIS

Max was ready to go and he grabbed his wallet and walked over to Alex's room. Knocked on the door and waited. The door opened and Alex walked out, shutting the door behind her.

Well hello. Glad to see you're all dried off now. Not that she really was but she had to play it cool.

Yeah that is what happens when you get a shower. No way of getting around it.

Yeah I guess so replied Alex. She smiled at him.

Once down at the restaurant they were able to seat themselves. A waitress came over with two menus and took their drink order.

So do you want to do the Whale watch today? Max was really wanting to do that.

Yeah that would be a good idea and then we can relax tomorrow. Alex really needed a few days to just relax. Hopefully they do not get a call before they leave.

The waitress came with the drinks and got their order for breakfast and left again.

Alex looked up on her phone the times that the whale watch was going on for that day. Hey, we can go this afternoon at two. I will call them and buy tickets after we eat. So what are we going to do until then? It is about a half hour away from here so we will have to drive there. Then we can go out somewhere on our way back for supper. Sounds good to you.

That sounds great. Well after breakfast we can go out to the beach, or to the pool. Maybe we can go in the jacuzzi.

Ooh that sounds good. Or we can go down after we get done with this and see if it is busy there before we go up and get changed.

Oh right. Yeah that would be a good idea. But it is nice out today so maybe it will be free.

It was after breakfast and Alex and Max went to check out the pool area. No one was there so they went up to their rooms and got changed. She was glad that she had showered earlier and her bathing suit was a two-piece. She bought it before the trip. She had brought a few of them but

MURDER IN THE NIGHT

this one was nice and she wanted to look nice in it. She changed and threw on a pair of shorts and grabbed a towel and went over to Max's room.

Well hello. Cute top. Do you have the matching bottoms to go with it under those shorts?

As a matter of fact I do smiled Alex. Come on lets go.

Ok. Max shut the door and they walked down to the pool area.

On their way down they saw a family with a child get on the elevator with them. The boy looked at them and asked them if they were married.

Alex replied, no we just work together and are here on a vacation.

Oh. replied the Boy. What's your name

Well my name is Alex and this is Max.

Hi.

The elevator had got to the floor that they were going to and opened. Everyone got off. The parents with the child went outside towards the beach. Max and Alex went towards the pool. She could not wait to get in and soak.

At the pool there was no one there still so it was nice to have the whole place to themselves.

Alex went over and set the timer on the jacuzzi and they both got in.

Ahh this is nice, replied Max.

Yes it is. I love to go in them. I am thinking of getting one myself.

Oh then you would never get rid of me. Max smiled when he said it.

You can come over anytime you want to get in and relax. Even if I am not there. You do not have to ask. It will be getting some use. But I have to get a cover for it.

Yeah to keep the leaves and stuff out of it.

Yes. I look at them everytime I see them set up somewhere.

Alex really was enjoying her time in the water. It felt good to be in it and feel relaxed. This is what she needed. This whole vacation is what she needed. At least she is not stressed and has to work long hours this week. This week is about her getting relaxed with her mind and body.

So what do you want to do for lunch? Not that I want to eat right now since we just ate. But just wanted to see what you want to do. And maybe we should go early to the Whale watch.

Yes I agree. I ordered the tickets on the phone and paid for them after lunch so that is all set. All we have to do is pick them up at the ticket counter.

Alex and Max were finally on their way to the Whale watch.

A two hour tour so that is really cool to see. Hopefully we can see a lot of whales close by. Alex was glad as she wanted to do this for so long.

I am sure we will be able to see a group of them. Max was hopeful.

As they drove up to the Whale watch parking lot there really were not a lot of cars there.

Wow looks like we will be able to move around on either side hopefully.

Yeah that will be good. I plan on taking pictures too while we are on the boat.

Me too. Alex was happy with just being able to go.

Alex walked up to the ticket booth and told her their name, she found the tickets and asked for identification.

Sure I have it. Alex pulled out her Drivers licence and gave it to the lady. She had to make sure that she was giving the right ticket to the right person.

Ok well we got our tickets and now we can go get on the boat.

Yeaaa. This is going to be so fun

Yes it is. Happy Memories. Alex would remember this for a long time.

Well, do you want a drink? They have a bar over there.

Sure whatever you are getting is fine with me.

Ok, be right back.

Alex went over by the edge to look out to see if she could see anything in the water but nothing yet.

Max came back with two glasses of wine and it was nice to have a friend to go whale watching with her. She only had a few friends that did things with her.

Max handed Alex a glass. The boat would be leaving soon once everyone had made it there. She could not wait to see the Whales.

I charged my phone so the battery is full so I will be able to get some great shots of the whales. She has been getting some pics of Max as well

MURDER IN THE NIGHT

while on the trip but he has no clue about it. She got a few pictures of him at the beach, at the pool area and while they were out shopping. They have so much in common and he is her perfect match. But someone with his perfection would never fall for her. She still had so much to work on with herself. How does someone love someone like her?

The boat's engineer that is running the Whale Watch for the day had made an announcement for all passengers to board the boat as it was getting ready to leave. More people started to board the boat.

Well good We are about to leave. I have been waiting to do this since I was younger and now I am able to do the whale watch. I have heard from many people that have gone and what kind of experience they have had when they went.

This is going to be fun I hope. Max stood by Alex as she sipped on her wine. Yes thank you for coming along and doing things with me. You're having a lot of fun.

Well I am very happy that I got to come along too because this trip has really been what I needed. I love the job and what we do and try to help those that need us to find out who did what but it is great to just get away to do something else. There is nothing like staying in a hotel. It is very relaxing, you do not have to worry about doing house work and to go down and have someone else cook for you is awesome. Max's excitement was showing. I need to do more of these trips as it is a great benefit for me. No wonder people love to travel.

Yes it really is refreshing. Just make plans on where you want to go and go from there. Always go to the hotels with the free breakfast. A hotel with a restaurant is even much more better because if you do not feel like leaving your hotel then you can stay right there and even order room service. And some places even deliver to the hotel as well.

This is another reason why I love my job. To be able to go and relax after or even when there is time to relax even if it is a few days. And you do not even have to leave your room if you do not want to. Just hang around in your hotel all day. I have actually done that once and it was nice. No one bothers me.

Ok well we are on our way. Alex was starting to get hot as it was supposed to get up to the eighties today and it felt hotter than that.

It was a half hour into the watch when they started to finally see the Whales. There were a few adults and their babies out swimming around. Alex was able to get several great pictures of them.

Hey, look over there. More are swimming around that way.

Oh wow. Alex got a few more pictures of the Whales swimming around in other areas. This was definitely a great day to do this. The whales coming out to be seen and swimming around the boat was the best feeling in the world. There were also a few dolphins swimming around as well. I guess that they do not want to be left out.

Max took out his phone and got some pictures of the Whales and he had also seen the Dolphins come around. The experience was so overwhelming to see and they both were happy to be able to do this.

Alex had managed to sneak in some pictures of Max watching the whales.

After the Watch was over Max and Alex went back towards the hotel. There was a sign for a Mexican Restaurant off of one of the other roads from the main road that they were on. So Alex turned down the road to find this place to eat. Mexican food was one of her favorites.

Mexican tonight huh? I like mexican. I sometimes make it at home for myself.

Oh yes I do too. Alex loved making Taco Salads. It was a great meal for the night after a long day at work.

Taco Ville was just down the road and Alex pulled in. It was busy. The smell from the restaurant was overwhelming. It smelled so good.

Max and Alex walked in and sat down at a booth. A waitress came over and handed them a menu. They both ordered a Coke and the waitress left.

Oh it smells wonderful here and look at the menu. It is full of choices. The drinks came and they still were not able to order as they had not figured out what they wanted. There were just so many different things. Finally picking out their dinner they talked about the whale watching trip.

The food came and Max and Alex went quiet eating their food.

MURDER IN THE NIGHT

Oh this is so good. I will have to make this taco bowl at home.

Yes it does look good, said Max.

How is your Burrito?

It is really good. So big. And the rice is good too.

They both went back to eating their food.

Back at the hotel Max and Alex went back up to Alex's room and sat out on the balcony.

Well this has been the best trip yet.

Yes it has. Max was watching the children play on the beach. A couple of children were building a sand castle city with a moat filled with water. The food trucks had lines of people. It was still warm out and Alex was glad that they were back resting. They talked for a while and then Max got up and went to his room. Alex changed clothes and laid on the bed to watch TV. She later fell asleep and did not wake up until morning.

152

Chapter Twenty-Five

There was a text message on her phone from Max. She looked at the time and saw that it was nine thirty. She texted Max back and got up to get a shower then called him.

Well hello there. Guess you were tired huh.

Yeah I was. I did not realize just how tired I was. I laid on the bed last night to watch a movie and fell asleep.

Did you have good dreams I hope?

Alex had to think. None of them were of him which she was sad about. Not really that great. Maybe I was too tired to dream. What about you?

I had a dream that I had a very successful business and we were busy. We even had a few other detectives working with us that were doing other cases. This is why I want to have more people on so that we can help more people.

That would be a great dream. We really do need more people. These cases are lasting longer than normal.

Yes, they are. Well, are you ready to go get breakfast?

Yes, I am. I am hungry this morning.

Ok, meet you in the hallway.

Alex went out and met Max in the hallway and they walked down to the elevator together.

How did you sleep last night?

I did not really wake up much or even stay awake for very long. It was a great night. Only would be better if it was with him.

There were several other people down eating breakfast as well. Children were talking about what they wanted to do for that day.

153

Max and Alex seated themselves next to a window.

Maybe I will order in for lunch replied Alex. If you want we can eat out on the balcony or eat at the table with the sliding door open. It's nice out so I want to enjoy it as much as I can.

Hey, that would be a good idea. Then maybe we could find a movie to watch. We do have snacks in our room and one of them was a bag of popcorn.

Oh yeah. I really have not had much of my snacks. But that would be a great idea.

Yeah, it is and I am glad that they put them in our rooms.

Yes, but we still have to pay for them after. They put it on the charge card after so it is not like it was part of the room deal.

Oh well, I can pay for what I ate. They actually refill the basket that the food is in every day when they come and make up the bed.

No, that is fine I got it. They already have my credit card number anyway so not a problem. So what movie do you want to watch? There is a list of movies in the paper on the desk that we can rent.

Oh, sure I can check them out. See what they have that we would both like.

The waitress came over and gave them two menus. Max and Alex both ordered coffee to drink.

Looking over the specials Alex found what she wanted to eat. She loved a good omelet.

I am going to get the Belgian waffle. I love them. And a couple of eggs on the side.

Ok, what about meat? Do you want meat?

No, I am going to go without the meat today. I need to watch what I eat as we have been eating all the good stuff these past few days. I do not want to gain too much because it is hard to lose weight after.

I understand. Maybe I should just go with the Veggie omelet. Maybe skip the home fries and bread.

The waitress came back with the coffee and also brought some water as well. Are you ready to order?

MURDER IN THE NIGHT

Sure, I will just take a veggie omelet. Nothing else to go with it. Thanks. And you sir.

Belgium waffle with two eggs sunny side up.

Ok, thanks.

So where were we? Let's just say that I am glad that we got to come here. It is so nice and not a run-of-the-mill hotel. It is actually one of the more expensive ones which make it nicer. That is why our rooms are nice and they have all of the fancy things in our room. I could have gotten the suite which has two bedrooms in it which I had almost got but someone else had booked it just as I was going to.

No, that's ok. Our rooms are nice. I love it here. The food is good, the hotel is beautiful and I love it because it is near the beach. I love watching the kids play and hear them laugh.

Yeah me too. Kid-friendly. I like the arcade section that they have here.

The waitress brought the food out? Here you go, is there anything else I can get you?

I am fine thanks, replied Alex. Max might want something.

Can I get some more creamer and coffee?

Sure. Will be right back.

After breakfast, Max and Alex went back up to her room. Max looked in the paper to see what movies were on and picked one. There is Halloween three. Would you want to watch that one?

Sure. That would be a good one to watch. Alex had already seen it but wanted to see it again.

Ok well I am going to go back over to my room for a minute and I will be right back.

Sure. Just don't close the door all the way so you can get back in.

Max left and Alex freshened up a bit while he was gone. She came out just as Max came back into the room.

I am just going to open the door to the balcony so that we can get some fresh air in here. We could watch the movie now instead of waiting till later.

Sure that would be great. You're not scared of scary movies are you?

Only if they scream or jump out on the screen. I mean I expect it to happen but I am never ready for it.

After the movie Alex and Max were sitting on the sofa really relaxed after the movie. Well I could go for a nap.

A nap? Yeah I guess I could go for one too. Max took the cue that she wanted to relax now. Well I could go to my room and leave you alone.

Why? The bed big enough for both of us? Alex had put on a big grin. Besides, I will behave.

Well, we will see about that. Max was ok with napping before getting something to eat later. Besides, he had not napped with anyone in a long time. And they are having a lazy day today so why not.

Ok good. Pick a side I don't care which side I sleep on.

Max and Alex got settled onto the bed. Alex could not believe that she had managed to get Max to lay down next to her. He smelled good and was breathing in the scent of him as much as she could without him noticing.

They both fell asleep.

An hour later Max managed to get up without disturbing Alex. He went back to his room and figured that Alex would call him later when she woke up.

Alex called around three in the afternoon. Max was laying down watching TV.

I woke up and you were gone.

Yeah, I slept for half an hour and so I just got up and came back here to relax.

Ok well, are you ready to go and get something to eat?

Sure, where do you want to go?

What about the restaurant downstairs again? That way we do not have to leave.

Yeah, we can do that. Just a lazy day today for me anyways. It's always nice to go and have fun but then it is nice to just come out and just relax without doing anything. Maybe go down and get in the hot tub again. We need to just have a few days of not really doing anything.

Murder in the Night

Are you ready to go now? Max was hungry.

Yes, I am ready. Alex brushed her hair and then walked out the door and met up with Max in the hallway.

It sure is quiet today.

Maybe most of the people had already gone home. Alex had not heard much for the past day. I think that the family with kids is gone.

Down at the restaurant Max and Alex walked in and were able to sit down at any table since they were not busy. Sometimes a hostess is there to seat people if it is busy.

They have a special of spaghetti and meatballs with salad and breadsticks.

That does sound good too. I think I am going to have that as well.

Max and Alex ordered their food and talked about what they wanted to do for the rest of the day and tomorrow since they had to leave the following day.

Well I think we could just go to the jacuzzi after but we have to wait until a while later.

Yeah that sounds like a great idea. And hopefully we will be able to sleep well tonight.

So what did you like best so far about the trip? asked Alex? Mine was the whale watching.

Same here. Watching them was really entertaining and a learning experience.

True. It is something that I would like to do again.

The waitress brought out their food. Neither one said anything for a while.

The food is really good, I am going to miss this place. Alex was happy with the food.

Yes it is good here. Beats eating alone at home.

After dinner they both went up to the room and got ready to go to the pool area. They were the only ones there which was nice. They have not seen the couple since the first day that they had met. Out of all the people that are here they thought that they would see them at least once since.

Well the jacuzzi was very inviting. They got in and sat in there for the limited time that they were supposed to be in. Then got out and sat at the table for a while and talked some more.

I wonder what the next case is going to be about, said Alex.

Not really sure. I was not able to get much information. We will find out when we go back. We have to go and talk to Jane, replied Max.

Ok well anyways I have to say that this has been a great time.

I think tomorrow we will have breakfast and then start to head home after. I really hate to go back as we have had a lot of fun and it just seemed to go bye so fast. But at least we have a place to look forward to coming back to. We can also check out other places to go to that are not as far away either. It's really hard to take time off right now because it is only the two of us. Until we get more people working with us. This will be good in case I have to make a trip back home for some reason, usually an emergency. My grandparents are getting older now and are needing help to get around.

Sure I understand. Family is important. Hopefully you know ahead of time so you can get there in time.

Chapter Twenty-Six

The next day Max and Alex had gone down for breakfast and then checked out of their rooms. Alex had to double check the room to make sure that she had everything packed. Sometimes you can miss something if you do not check again.

Well time to go. It was a fun ride while it lasted.

Yeah, Max looked around and told the girl at the desk that they had a great time and that they would be back again.

Great, I am glad that you both liked it here. We enjoyed having you here.

Thank you, replied Alex.

They both went out and loaded up the car and went on their way back home.

Well this was a really great place to get away to. I will definitely have to come back here. Hopefully we can or I can come back next year.

You can count on it, replied Alex. We can stop for lunch on our way home when we are close to home. That way we do not have to make something. I have a lot to get done before tomorrow.

So do I. I also need to get laundry done. The apartment is clean at least when I get home. And I have to stop and pick up milk and bread.

Same. We can stop on the way to my place because I do not want to have to leave again.

Great. I will get the groceries at the store. You brought me there and back.

That is fine and really no problem. I am just so happy that we both got to go. We will have to find more places to go to because I love to actually travel around and see new places.

PEGGY HARGIS

I am usually a homebody but this is good for my mental health. Max knows that the job can get crazy and very depressing. It is always good to get away and forget about what has happened. The real world is getting too complicated lately.

You're right. I have known several people in my life that have taken their own life. They just felt like that was the only way out. But really there are other things to do to get out of the depression mode. This is why I like to go places. You have to.

I know. Depression is nothing to just try to get through. It is rough on everyone and I am sure that everyone tends to get depressed once in a while. I lost one of my best friends because of it. I was in middle school. Things happened that even he could not help his friend with. Then one day he went home from school and that was the last time he saw him alive.

So the best thing to do is to go away and do something fun to get through the tough times, said Alex. If it was not for hotels and getting away from it all I don't know what I would do. There is just so much to see and do out in the real world.

So where do you want to go next time asked Max? He loved to go just as much as I did and he was just so easy going at doing whatever there was to do that was fun. He is the most perfect person to go and hang out with.

Well we will have to figure that out later on. Also depends on if we are able to, depending on how long this case is going to be. We might be able to go on an overnight stay somewhere. That could also be fun. I have done a few of those also.

Ooh ok. Max smiled and we talked all the way home about future plans.

THE END